# Larry McMurtry

# BOONE'S LICK

## LICK

A NOVEL

SCRIBNER PAPERBACK FICTION
Published by Simon & Schuster
NEW YORK LONDON TORONTO SYDNEY SINGAPORE

SCRIBNER PAPERBACK FICTION
Simon & Schuster, Inc.
Rockefeller Center
1230 Avenue of the Americas
New York, NY 10020

First Scribner Paperback Fiction edition 2001

SCRIBNER PAPERBACK FICTION and design are trademarks of Macmillan Library Reference USA, Inc., used under license by Simon & Schuster, the publisher of this work.

For information regarding special discounts for bulk purchases, please contact Simon & Schuster Special Sales at 1-800-456-6798 or *business@simonandschuster.com*

Designed by Karolina Harris

Manufactured in the United States of America

10 9 8 7 6 5 4 3 2 1

The Library of Congress has cataloged the Simon & Schuster edition as follows:
McMurtry, Larry.
Boone's Lick : a novel / Larry McMurtry.
p. cm.
I. Title.
PS3563.A319 B6 2000
813'.54—dc21     00-056342

ISBN 0-684-86886-5
0-7432-1627-X (Pbk)

# BOOK I
# Mules

**1** U N C L E  Seth was firmly convinced
that bad things mostly happen on
cloudy days.

"A thunderhead or two don't hurt, but too much
cloudy weather makes people restless and mean, females particularly," he remarked, as we were walking down to the Missouri River.

"They don't make Ma mean, she's mean anyway," G.T. said—he had acquired the habit of con-
tradiction, as Uncle Seth liked to put it. G.T. could
usually be counted on to do the unexpected: only
yesterday he jumped up and stabbed Granpa
Crackenthorpe in the leg with a pocketknife, probably because he got tired of hearing Granpa complain about the food. The knife didn't go in very
far, but even so, Granpa's pallet looked as if a shoat

had been butchered on it. G.T. ran away and hid in the thicket, but Ma gave him a good thrashing anyway, when he finally came in. Quick tempered as he was, G.T. was still scared of the dark.

"It's best to walk small around Mary Margaret," Uncle Seth allowed. "You just need to walk a little smaller on cloudy days."

The three of us had strolled down to the river in hopes that we could catch or trap or shoot something Ma could cook—something with a good taste to it, if possible. We had been living on old dry mush for about three weeks, which is why Granpa complained. I had a fishing pole, G.T. had a wire-mesh crawdad trap, and Uncle Seth had his Sharps rifle, which he kept in an oilcloth sheath, never allowing a drop of rain to touch it. He had been a Union sharpshooter in the war between the states and could regularly pop a turtle in the head at seventy-five yards, a skill but not a useful skill, because the turtles he popped always sank. If anybody got to eat them, it was only other turtles.

The clouds hung low and heavy over the big muddy river that day; they were as dull colored as felt. It was just the kind of weather most likely to cause Uncle Seth to dwell on calamities he had experienced in the past.

"It was nearly this cloudy that day in Richmond when I tripped over that goddamn wagon tongue and shot off half my kneecap," he reminded us. "If the sun had been shining I would have been alert enough to step over that wagon tongue. It was the day after the war ended. I had no need of a rifle, but that gloomy weather made me fearful. I got it in my head that there might be a Reb or two in the neighborhood—a Reb who hadn't heard the good news."

"If the war had just been over one day, then there might have been," I said. It seemed reasonable to me.

"Son, there wasn't a Reb within thirty-five miles of us that day," Uncle Seth said. "I could have left my rifle in the tent, but I didn't, and the upshot of it is that I'll be gimpy for the rest of my life."

G.T. had just eased his crawdad trap into the water, near the muddy shore.

"If you'd shut up I might catch some crawdads," he said.

"Why, crawdads can't hear," Uncle Seth said. "You sass your elders too much, G.T. A boy that starts off sassing his elders is apt to end up on the wrong end of a hang rope—at best you can look forward to a long stretch in the territorial prison."

He was a tall, fidgety man, Uncle Seth. No part of him was ever really still—not unless he was dead drunk, a not unusual condition for him. Pa said there was a time when Seth Cecil could walk faster and keep walking longer than any man on the plains; of course, that was before the accident, when Pa and Uncle Seth were partners in the freighting business, hauling goods from the Missouri River to the forts up in the north. Even now, with half a kneecap, Uncle Seth wasn't what you'd call *slow*. He could still manage a pretty long stride, if he had some reason to be in a hurry—it irked him that Pa, who was his younger brother, made him a stay-at-home partner, rather than letting him go upriver with the freight. I think it irked him so much that he and Pa might have come to blows, if Ma hadn't made it plain that she would only tolerate so much, when it came to family quarrels.

"I can still drive a wagon, you know, Dickie," Uncle Seth pointed out, the last time Pa was home. "Hauling freight ain't that complicated."

"I know you can manage a wagon, but could you outrun a Blackfoot Indian, if it came to a footrace?" Pa asked. "I doubt you could even outrun a Potawatomi, if it was a long footrace."

"Why would I need to outrun a Potawatomi, or a Blackfoot either?" Uncle Seth asked. "I admit I'd be in trouble if a bunch of them closed in on me, but then, so would you."

G.T. didn't really have the patience to be a good crawdad fisherman. Ten minutes was all he gave it before pulling his trap out. It held one crawdad— not a very large one.

"One crawdad won't go far," he said. "I expect there are a million crawdads in the Missouri River, and here I ain't caught but one."

"They ain't in the river, they're in that slimy mud," Uncle Seth pointed out—it was just then that we heard a gunshot from the direction of the house.

"That was a rifle shot," Uncle Seth said. "I expect Mary Margaret finally drew a bead on that big bobcat that's been snatching her chickens."

"You're wrong again," G.T. said, pointing toward the house. "Sis wouldn't be running that fast if it was just a bobcat."

G.T. didn't exaggerate about Neva's speed. She was fairly flying down the trail. Neva was only fourteen but she had been long legged enough to outrun anybody in the family—even Pa—for the last two or three years. When our smokehouse caught on fire Neva ran all the way into Boone's Lick before any of us could even find a bucket, and was soon back with a passel of drunks willing to try and put the fire out. Fortunately, it wasn't much of a fire—all we lost was an old churn somebody had left in the smokehouse.

Still, everybody who saw Neva go flying down the road that day talked about her run for years—some even wanted to take her to St. Louis and enter her in a footrace, but that plan fell through.

"Who do they think they're going to find in St. Louis who wants to run a footrace with a little girl from Boone's Lick?" Uncle Seth asked at the time, a question that stumped the town.

This time Neva arrived at the river so out of breath that she had to gulp in air for a while before she could talk.

"She's outrun her own voice," G.T. said. He was slow of foot himself, and very impressed by Neva's speed.

"Easy girl, easy girl," Uncle Seth said, as if he was talking to a nervous filly.

"It's a big bunch of thieves!" Neva gasped, finally. "They're stealing our mules—ever one of our mules."

"Why, the damned ruffians!" Uncle Seth said. A red vein popped out along the top of his nose—that red vein nearly always popped out when he got anxious or mad.

"We heard a shot," he said. "I hope nobody ain't shot your Ma." He said it in a worried voice, too. Despite what he said about women and clouds, we all knew that Uncle Seth was mighty partial to Ma.

"No, it was Ma that shot," Neva said. "She killed a horse."

"Oh—good," he said. "The world can spare a horse, but none of us can spare your mother."

"Gimme your rifle, I'll go kill them all," G.T. said, but when he tried to grab the Sharps, Uncle Seth snatched it back.

He looked downriver for a moment. Boone's Lick was only half a mile away. He seemed to be trying to decide who to send for help, Neva or me. G.T. had already started for the house, with his crawdad trap and his one crawdad. G.T. wasn't about to give up his one crawdad.

"Honey, when you catch your breath maybe you ought to run on down to Boone's Lick and bring Sheriff Stone back with you," Uncle Seth said. "It's the sheriff's job to deal with horse theft, and mule theft too."

"I don't need to bring the sheriff, because he's already there," Neva said. "It was the sheriff's horse Ma shot."

"Uh-oh. Where was Sheriff Stone at the time?" Uncle Seth asked.

"Sitting on his horse," Neva said, in a tone that suggested she considered it a pretty stupid question. "It fell over when Ma shot it and nearly mashed his leg."

Uncle Seth absorbed this information calmly. If he was surprised, he didn't show it.

"Oh, I see, honey," he said. "It's Baldy Stone that's stealing our mules. I guess that's just the kind of law you have to expect in Missouri. Let's go wade into them, Shay."

I *was* surprised that Ma had shot the sheriff's horse, but my opinion wasn't asked.

"Do you still want me to go to Boone's Lick?" Neva asked, as Uncle Seth and I started for the house.

"Why, no, honey—no reason to run your legs off," Uncle Seth said. "The law's already at the freight yard—who would you get if you were to go to Boone's Lick?"

"Wild Bill Hickok," Neva said—it was clear she had already thought the matter out.

"He's usually in the saloon," she added. I saw right then, from the look on her face, that she intended to go see Wild Bill, whatever Uncle Seth advised. Neva might be young, but she had Ma's determination, and there were not many people, young or old, male or female, with more determination than Ma.

"I'm impressed by your steady thinking, honey," Uncle Seth said. "Bill could be a big help, if he was in the mood to be, but this cloudy weather might have put him off."

"You're the only one that minds clouds," Neva said. She had got her wind back and looked ready for a tussle.

"If there weren't no clouds it would never rain, and if it didn't rain nothing would grow, and if nothing grew, then the animals would all starve, and then *we'd* starve," Neva said, giving Uncle Seth one of her cool looks.

Uncle Seth didn't say anything. He saw that Neva had backed him into a pretty tight corner, where cloudy weather was concerned. G.T. was already halfway to the house, too.

"A *pistolero* like Bill Hickok is likely to have his moods, whatever the weather," he said. "I try not to interfere with Bill and he tries not to interfere with me. I think we better just go home and see why Baldy Stone thinks he has the right to requisition our mules."

Neva immediately started trotting down the riverbank toward Boone's Lick. I wasn't surprised, and neither was Uncle Seth.

"There's no shortage of hardheaded women in the Cecil family," he said, mildly. "If you hit one of them in the head with a rock it would break the rock."

Our cabin wasn't far from the river. Pa and Uncle Seth had been raised on the Mississippi River, in the Ioway country; both of them lived by rivers until their hauling business forced them out onto the plains from time to time. Despite his gimpy knee Uncle Seth was only a step behind me when we came around the chicken yard. There was no sign of Ma, and no sign of our mules, either, but there was plenty of sign of Sheriff Baldy Stone, a short man who had grown very round in the course of his life.

Sheriff Baldy was trying to unsaddle his dead horse, a large roan animal who had fallen about twenty steps from our cabin door. It was a big horse. The sheriff had the girth unbuckled but when he tried to pull the cinch out from under the horse it wouldn't budge.

G.T., who had beat us home by a good margin, was standing nearby, but he didn't offer to help. After tugging at the cinch several times without having any effect, Sheriff Baldy abruptly gave up and sat down on the corpse of his horse to take a breather. He was almost as out of breath as Neva had been when she showed up down by the river.

After resting for a minute, the sheriff looked up at Uncle Seth and gave a little wave—or it may have been a salute. The sheriff had only been a corporal in the war, whereas Uncle Seth had been a captain.

"Well, Seth, she shot my horse and here I sit," Sheriff Baldy said. "Do you realize I courted Mary Margaret once, when things were different?"

"I've heard that rumor—I expect she still has a sweet spot for you, Baldy," Uncle Seth said.

"A sweet spot? I don't think so," the sheriff said.

"It would explain why she shot the horse and not you," Uncle Seth pointed out.

The remark struck G.T. as funny. He began to cackle, which drew a frown from the sheriff. Just then Ma came out the door, with the baby in her arms. The baby, a girl named Marcy, was cooing and blowing little spit bubbles. Ma handed her right over to Uncle Seth, at which point Marcy began to coo even louder. Pa was so busy upriver that he hadn't even been home to see the baby yet—for all little Marcy knew, Uncle Seth was her pa, if she even knew what a pa was, at that age.

"Now, Mary Margaret," Uncle Seth said, "you oughtn't to have handed me this child. There might be gunplay to come, depending on how mad Baldy is and what he's done with our mules."

"No gunplay, no gunplay," Sheriff Baldy said. "Getting my horse shot out from under me is violence enough for one afternoon. You can hold ten babies if you want to, Seth."

Ma walked around the dead horse, looking down at it thoughtfully. She didn't say a word, either kind or unkind, to Sheriff Baldy. When she got round to the rump of the horse she leaned over and tested it with her fingers, to see if it might have a little fat on it, rather than just being all muscular and stringy.

"Why, it *is* a horse. That's a surprise," Ma said lightly.

"Of course it's a horse, thoroughly dead!" the sheriff said. "You shot it out from under me before I could even open my mouth to ask for the loan of your mules. What did you think it was, if not a horse?"

"An elk," Ma said, with a kind of faraway look in her eye. "I thought it was a big fat elk, walking right up to my door."

She paused. She had lost flesh in the years of the war—everybody had.

"I thought, no more mush, we're going to be eating elk," she said. "Granpa can stop complaining and I can be making a little richer milk for this baby—she's not as chubby as my other babies have been."

Sheriff Baldy sat there on the dead horse with his mouth open—a bug could have flown right into his mouth, if one had been nearby.

"You mean you didn't shoot it because we were borrowing the mules?" he asked. "I was going to explain why we needed the mules, but you didn't give me time. You stepped out the door and the next thing I knew this horse was dead."

Ma made no reply—she just tested the rump in another place with her fingers. Baby Marcy was still bubbling and cooing.

"Well, I swear, Mary Margaret," Sheriff Baldy said. "This was a big roan horse. How could you get it in your head that it was an elk?"

Ma still had the faraway look in her eye. It worried me when she got that look, though I couldn't really have said what it was I was worried about. I think it must have worried the sheriff too.

"I guess I was just too hungry to see straight, Eddie," she said, calling Sheriff Baldy by his first name. At least I guess it was his first name. I had never heard anyone use it before.

"I'm hungry and my family's hungry," Ma went on. "Horse meat's not as tasty as elk, but it will do. Whatever I owe you we can put toward the rent of the mules."

She started for the house, but the look on the sheriff's face must have made her feel a little sorry for him, because she turned at the cabin door and looked back at him for a moment.

"We've got a little buttermilk to spare, Eddie, if you'd like some," she said, as she opened the door.

"I'll take the buttermilk," Sheriff Baldy said.

He got off the dead horse and we all followed Ma through the door.

**2** GRANPA Crackenthorpe got up from his pallet when we all trooped in. I think he was hoping for a dipper of buttermilk, but he didn't get one. There was only one dipperful left in the crock—while the sheriff was enjoying it Granpa began to get annoyed.

"I'm the oldest—that was my buttermilk," Granpa said. "I was planning to have it later, with my mush."

"Hubert don't like me—I've arrested him too often," Sheriff Baldy remarked, wiping a little line of buttermilk off his upper lip.

Granpa, who didn't have much of a bladder left, had formed the awkward habit of pissing in public, if he happened to be in public when the need arose. Sometimes he made it into the saloon and peed in

the spittoons, but sometimes he didn't make it
that far, and those were the times when Sheriff
Baldy had felt it best to arrest him.

"Hubert, we've got enough troubles in Boone's
Lick without having to tolerate public pissing," the
sheriff said. "If you've got a minute, Seth, I'll explain why I took the mules."

"Fine, but if it's not too much to ask, we need to
borrow one of them back for a few minutes," Uncle
Seth said. "Otherwise we'll have to butcher that
roan horse practically in Mary Margaret's front
room, which is sure to bring flies. If we could borrow a mule back for half an hour we could drag the
carcass over to the butchering tree."

"That's fair—the boys just took them down to
the livery stable," the sheriff said. "If one of these
young fellows can go fetch one, then when you're
done with your dragging I can ride the mule back
to town."

"G.T., go," Ma said, and G.T. went. Ma already
had the whetstone out and was getting ready to
sharpen a couple of butcher knives.

"I'm the oldest but nobody's listening to me,"
Granpa Crackenthorpe said—a true statement. No
one paid him the slightest mind.

"It's that gang over at Stumptown—the
Millers," Sheriff Baldy said. "The war's been over
nearly fourteen months but you couldn't tell it if
you happen to wander over to Stumptown. The
Millers are robbing every traveler they can catch,
and killing quite a few of them."

"I don't doubt it—Jake Miller's as mean as a

pig, but what's it got to do with our mules?" Uncle Seth inquired.

"I'm going over there and clean out the Millers," the sheriff said. "You know how poorly all the horseflesh is around here. The farmers all quit, because of the war. Mary Margaret just killed the only good horse in Boone's Lick."

"I thought it was an elk," Ma said firmly, as if that subject had been disposed of forever.

The sheriff just sighed.

"If the Millers see somebody passing through on a decent horse they kill the rider and take the horse," the sheriff said.

Right there I saw the sheriff's point—he was right about the poor horseflesh around Boone's Lick. But Pa and Uncle Seth were in the hauling business—they couldn't afford sickly mules. Uncle Seth went up to Ioway himself and brought back fodder for our mules. There hadn't been much fighting in Ioway; the farmers there were happy to sell what they had to Uncle Seth, the result being that our mules were the best-conditioned animals anywhere around Boone's Lick. No wonder the sheriff wanted to borrow them, if he had a hard job to do.

Ma was whetting her knives, which made such a racket that the rest of us went outside.

"I guess I can't blame you for wanting your posse to have decent mounts," Uncle Seth said to Sheriff Baldy. "That's correct thinking, as far as it goes, but it don't go far enough."

Sheriff Baldy just looked at him. It might be that the shock of having his horse shot out from under him by a woman he had once courted had just hit him. His mouth hung open again, inviting flies and bugs.

"Of course, I have no objection to you borrowing our mules for a patriotic expedition, provided the expedition is well planned," Uncle Seth said. "How many posse men have you signed up so far?"

"One, so far," the sheriff admitted.

"Uh-oh, there's the incorrect part of your thinking," Uncle Seth said. "There's a passel of Millers, and Jake ain't the only one that's mean. If you go wandering over there with an inadequate force our mules will be at risk. Jake Miller can spot a valuable mule as quick as the next man."

"I know that," Sheriff Baldy said. He looked a little discouraged.

"I expect you were counting on our fine mules to attract a posse," Uncle Seth said. "It might work, too. At least, it might if you're offering cash payment too."

"I can offer five dollars a man, and fifty dollars to Wild Bill Hickok, if he'll come," the sheriff said.

Something about that remark irked Uncle Seth, because the red vein popped out again on his nose. I don't think the sheriff noticed.

"You mean if I was to join your posse you'd offer me forty-five dollars less than you're offering Bill Hickok to do the same job, even though the two of us were commanded by General Phil Sheridan and *I* was the sharpshooter and Bill just a common spy?" Uncle Seth inquired.

It didn't take the sheriff but a second to figure out what he had done wrong.

"Why, Seth, I never supposed you'd want to join a posse," he said.

"For fifty dollars I'll join it and enlist Shay and G.T. too," Uncle Seth said. "The boys will work for nothing, of course."

That remark startled me so that if I had been sitting on a fence I expect I would have fallen off. Ma wouldn't hear of our fighting in the war, though plenty of fourteen- and fifteen-year-olds *did* fight in it; and now Uncle Seth, with no discussion, was offering to trot us off to Stumptown to take on the notorious Miller gang, an outfit filled with celebrated killers: Cut-Nose Jones, Little Billy Perkins, and the four violent Millers themselves.

The sheriff didn't immediately respond to Uncle Seth's offer, but he didn't immediately reject it, either.

"If I had you and Hickok and the two boys and myself, I don't suppose I'd need much more of a posse," he finally said.

"That's right, you wouldn't," Uncle Seth said. "Here comes G.T., leading Old Sam. Old Sam could pull a house up a hill, if somebody hitched him to it."

Sheriff Baldy still looked worried.

"There's two problems, Seth," he said.

Before Uncle Seth could ask what they were Ma came outside and stuck little Marcy in his arms again.

"You keep running off and leaving this baby," she said. "I can't have a baby around when I'm sharpening knives."

Little Marcy was still in a perfectly good humor.

She began to wave her arms and kick her feet.

"What were the two problems, Baldy?" Uncle Seth said. He looked a little put upon.

"A hundred dollars is a lot to pay for a posse," the sheriff said. "We could build a new city hall for a hundred dollars."

"Yes, but once you got it built you'd still have the Millers to worry with," Uncle Seth pointed out. "What's problem number two?"

"I haven't asked Hickok yet," the sheriff admitted. "That's problem number two."

"Then go ask him," Uncle Seth advised. He strolled over my way, meaning to stick me with Marcy, but I sidestepped him. Marcy didn't like me near as much as she liked Uncle Seth. If I took her she would be bawling within a minute, which would make it hard to listen to the conversation.

"I'm scared to ask him, Seth," the sheriff said. "I ain't a bit scared of Jake Miller but the mere sight of Billy Hickok makes me quake in my boots."

G.T. arrived with Old Sam and I helped him tie on to the dead horse, after which Old Sam dragged the big roan gelding over to the butchering tree, freeing the sheriff's saddle in the process.

"Would you mind asking him for me, Seth, since the two of you are old friends?" the sheriff said.

"'Old friends' might be putting it a little too strongly, but I don't mind asking him to help out," Uncle Seth said. "I'll do it as soon as I can get shut of this baby girl, which might not be until tomorrow, the way things are looking."

"Tomorrow would be fine," Sheriff Baldy said.

**3** O N C E  we got the carcass of the big roan hitched up to a good stout limb of the butchering tree, Sheriff Baldy threw his saddle on Old Sam and rode back down to Boone's Lick.

"Please don't forget about Bill Hickok, Seth," he said, before he left. "The Millers ain't getting nicer, they're getting meaner."

Uncle Seth just waved. I don't think he was too pleased about his commission, but I had no time to dwell on the matter. The horse had just seemed to be a horse when Old Sam was dragging his carcass off, but by the time we had been butchering for thirty minutes it felt like we had a dead elephant on our hands. Ma worked neat, but G.T. had never known neat from dirty. By the time he got the horse's leg unjointed he was so bloody that Ma tried to get him to take his clothes off and work naked, a suggestion that shocked him.

The sight of G.T. shocked Granpa Crackenthorpe too, when he tottered out to give us a few instructions. Granpa Crackenthorpe liked to comment that he had long since forgotten more useful things than most people would ever know. He claimed to be expert at butchering horseflesh, but the sight of G.T., bloody from head to foot, shocked him so that he completely lost track of whatever instructions he had meant to give us.

"I was in the battle of the Bad Axe River," he remarked. "That was when we killed off most of the Sauk Indians and quite a few of the Fox Indians too. The Mississippi River was red as a ribbon that day, from all the Indian blood in it, but it wasn't no redder than G.T. here."

"That's right," Ma said. "He's ruined a perfectly good shirt. I tried to get him to undress before he started hacking, but I guess he's too modest to think about saving his clothes."

"Ma!" G.T. said—he could not accept the thought of nakedness.

I was put in charge of the gut tubs. It was plain that Ma didn't intend to waste an ounce of that horse—she even cracked the bones and scraped out the marrow. Of course, it had been a hungry month—Ma hadn't even allowed us to kill a chicken.

"A chicken is just an egg-laying machine," she pointed out. "We can live on eggs if we have to, although I'd rather not."

Uncle Seth didn't help us with the butchering, not one bit. He rarely turned his hand to mundane labor—this irritated G.T. but didn't seem to bother Ma.

"Somebody's got to watch Marcy, and Neva ain't here to do it," Ma said, when G.T. complained about Uncle Seth not helping.

I will say that Uncle Seth was good with babies. Marcy never so much as whimpered, the whole afternoon. Once Ma had the meat cut into strips for smoking she stopped long enough to nurse Marcy. Uncle Seth seemed to be lost in thought—he often got his lost-in-thought look when he was afraid somebody was going to ask him to do something he didn't want to do. When Ma finished nursing she handed the baby back to him and took up her butcher knife again. She didn't say a word.

All afternoon, while Ma and G.T. and I worked, skinning that horse, stripping the guts, cutting up what Ma meant to cook right away, and salting down the rest, I kept having the feeling that I was putting off thinking about something. If I hadn't had such a bunch of work to do I would have been lost in thought myself, like Uncle Seth.

What I was putting off thinking about was Ma's plain statement that she thought the horse was an elk. Up to that point in life I had thought my mother was a truthful woman. So far as I knew she was the most truthful person on earth, and the most perfect. Pa didn't really even try to be truthful, and though Uncle Seth may have tried to be truthful from time to time, we all knew he couldn't really manage it. He favored a good story over a dull truth anytime, and everybody knew it.

Ma, though, was different. She always told the truth, whether it was pleasant or unpleasant—and it was pretty unpleasant a lot of the time. An example of the unpleasant side was the day when she told Granpa that if he didn't stop walking around with his pants down in front of Neva she was going to take him to Boone's Lick and leave him to beg for a living: and Granpa was her own father!

"You can cover yourself or you can leave," she told him—and after that Granpa took care to cover himself.

But now I had, with my own ears, just heard Ma say that she had thought a horse was an elk. How could a person with two good eyes think a horse was an elk? Did Ma consider that we were so desperate for vittles that she had to lie—or, when she looked out the door, did her eyes really turn a horse into an elk, in her sight? Was my Ma a liar, or was she crazy? And if she had gone crazy, where did that leave me and G.T. and baby Marcy and Granpa and Uncle Seth? All of us depended on Ma. If she was crazy, what would we do?

As the afternoon went on and the butchering slowly got done, I began to wonder if the reason Uncle Seth seemed so lost in thought was because he was asking himself the same question. If Ma was crazy, what would we all do?

Not that Ma *seemed* crazy—not a bit of it. Once the butchering was finished for the day—there was still sausage making to think about—Ma cooked up a bunch of horse meat cutlets and we had all the meat we wanted for the first time since the war ended; meat just seemed to get real scarce in Missouri, about the time the war ended.

"Have you ever eaten a mule, Seth?" Ma asked, while we were all tying into the cutlets.

"No—never been quite that desperate," Uncle Seth said. "I suppose a fat mule would probably be about as tasty as a skinny horse, though."

"Maybe," Ma said, and then she suddenly looked around the table and realized Neva was missing.

"Where's Neva?" she asked. "I've been so busy cutting up Eddie's horse that I forget about my own daughter. I sent her to fetch you, Seth. Where'd she go?"

Then her eyes began to rake back and forth, from G.T. to me and back.

"I thought I trained you boys to look after your little sister better than this," Ma said.

"Oh, she went trotting off to Boone's Lick," Uncle Seth said. "I got so busy tending to this baby that I forgot about her."

There was a silence—not a nice silence, though.

"She probably found a little girlfriend and is skipping rope or rolling a hoop or something," Uncle Seth suggested.

Ma looked at me and snapped her fingers. "Shay, go," she said.

I got up immediately and G.T. did too, but Ma snapped her fingers again and G.T. sat back down—not that he was happy about it.

"Why can't I go?" he asked, a question that Ma ignored.

"I'll stroll along with the boy," Uncle Seth said, getting up from the table. "I need to see Bill Hickok about something anyway."

Ma didn't look happy to hear that.

"I thought he left," she said.

"Not as of today, according to the sheriff," Uncle Seth said.

"Then that explains where Neva is, doesn't it?" Ma said.

Her tone of voice upset Granpa Crackenthorpe so much that he got his big cap-and-ball pistol and wandered off out the door.

"I believe there's a panther around—I better take care of it," he said. That was always Granpa's excuse, when things got tense at the table. I had never seen a panther in my whole life and neither had G.T. But the notion that a panther was about to get the mules was the method Granpa used when he wanted to stand clear of trouble.

Ma paid him no mind. Now it seemed to be her turn to be lost in thought.

"Now, Mary Margaret, you don't need to be worrying about Neva," Uncle Seth said. "If she should happen to be with Bill Hickok then she's as safe as if she was in jail. Bill is a perfect gentleman where young ladies are concerned."

Ma didn't answer him. She got up and followed us to the door, but she didn't come outside.

"Hurry back," she said, as we started down the road.

**4** O N C E we started on the road to town I couldn't hold back my question.

"That was a horse we butchered," I said. "It wasn't an elk."

"Well, I didn't do any of the butchering but it did seem to have the appearance of a horse," Uncle Seth agreed.

"Besides that, Sheriff Baldy was sitting on the horse," I reminded him. "Even if Ma thought a horse looked like an elk, there was the sheriff on top of it. A sheriff wouldn't ride an elk."

"It would be unlikely, particularly if it was Baldy," Uncle Seth agreed.

To my disappointment, he didn't seem to want to talk about the fact that Ma had confused a horse with an elk—or had claimed to, at least. Maybe it was because he was thinking about Wild Bill Hickok, the famous *pistolero* we were going to see. I had heard him talk about Wild Bill once or twice, so I knew the two men knew one another—but that was all I knew. Uncle Seth had picked up his rifle as we left the house—it was still in its oilcloth sheath. I don't think he brought it along because he was worried about panthers, either. I didn't know what he might be worried about. Uncle Seth gambled a lot—he might owe Mr. Hickok money, for all I knew. It could even be money he didn't have. Or Hickok might owe *him* money, in which case getting him to pay might not be easy.

I had no idea what Uncle Seth might be thinking, but then, suddenly, he told me.

"I like the Cheyenne," he said. You never knew when Uncle Seth would change the subject.

I had never met a Cheyenne, so had no opinion to give.

"I would trust a Cheyenne over a Frenchman, most days," he went on. "The Cheyenne rarely cheat you more than you can afford to be cheated. That's why I like to trade with them."

I didn't say anything. I knew Uncle Seth would get around to telling me what he wanted to tell me if I could be patient and hold my tongue.

I think he was about ready to come out with it when we saw somebody come slipping up the road—the somebody was Neva.

"Hello," Uncle Seth said. "It's nice to see you're well."

He could see her clearly, because the clouds had

finally blown away and there was a big bright moon.

"Hello," Neva said, and that was all she said. She went right on past us, toward the freight yard. If she had any adventures in Boone's Lick she didn't share them with us.

"Say, look out for Granpa," Uncle Seth called after her. "He's out with his old cap-and-ball again, looking for panthers. Don't yowl or he might shoot you."

"I don't never yowl," Neva said. "Anyway, I don't think that old pistol of his will even shoot."

Then she was gone.

"Besides being hardheaded, the womenfolk in this family are closemouthed, too," he said. "The only way you're going to know what one of them does is if you catch her at it."

Then he didn't say anything for a while, and we were nearly to town.

"What was that you were saying about the Cheyenne Indians?" I asked. I was determined to find out *something,* even if it wasn't anything I particularly wanted to know.

"Oh, I was thinking about that elk Mary Margaret claims she saw," Uncle Seth said. "The Cheyenne explanation would be that there was an elk somewhere who realized that us Cecils were getting poorly from being so underfed. The elk might have been an old elk, who had been thinking about dying anyway. So the elk decided to give it up, so we could have some proper vittles for a while. Baldy Stone came along and the elk put his spirit into the horse Baldy was riding. It looked like a horse but Mary Margaret seen deeper and realized it was an elk. So she shot it, just like she said. If you ask her thirty years from now what she shot that day Baldy and his deputies requisitioned the mules, she'd still say she shot an elk. And if you believe like the Cheyenne believe, then she was right."

"But there are no elk around here," I pointed out.

"No, but there are a few left in Kansas," Uncle Seth said. "That's probably where it came from—Kansas."

The explanation took me by surprise—I didn't know what to think about it.

"But Ma ain't a Cheyenne Indian," I mentioned.

"Women and Indians are a lot alike," Uncle Seth assured me. "In some ways they are *just* alike."

"Then Ma didn't lie?" I asked.

"Oh no—Mary Margaret don't lie," Uncle Seth said. "She seen an elk, just like she told the sheriff."

"You don't think it could mean Ma's crazy?" I asked.

Uncle Seth looked at me as if *I* was the one who might be crazy, for even considering such a thing.

"No, Mary Margaret ain't crazy, any more than the Cheyenne Indians are crazy—at least most of them ain't," he said.

By then we were smack in the middle of Boone's Lick, right outside the saloon.

**5** W I L D Bill Hickok sat at a table at the back of the saloon, smoking a thin cigar. He wore a buckskin jacket a lot like the one Pa wore, only Pa's was always filthy from buffalo grease or bear grease or something, whereas Wild Bill's looked as if it had just come from the tailor. He was playing a hand of solitaire when we walked in, his chair tilted back a little.

I guess he made it clear that he didn't want company, because there was nobody at any of the tables just in front of him. All of the customers were either crowded up at three or four tables near the front of the saloon or else were standing at the bar.

Uncle Seth didn't let the empty tables stop him.

"Why, hello, Seth," Mr. Hickok said, when we approached his table. "You're still keeping your plinking rifle safe from the damp, I see."

"Hello, Bill," Uncle Seth said. "This hulking lad is my nephew Sherman—Shay for short."

To my shock Mr. Hickok settled his chair, stood up, smiled, and shook hands with me courteously.

"He's no kin of William Tecumseh Sherman, your former commander—or was he your former commander?" Uncle Seth asked.

"No, the little frizzy-hair terrier never got to order me around," Mr. Hickok said. "The two of you can have a seat."

I noticed when I was taking a chair that several of the fellows crowded up in the front of the saloon were looking daggers at us—they didn't like it that we got to sit with Mr. Hickok and they just got to sit with their ugly selves. Uncle Seth didn't give them a thought.

"We had a spot of trouble earlier in the day," Uncle Seth said. "I believe my niece may have stopped by to talk to you about it."

"Oh yes, Miss Geneva," Mr. Hickok said. "She's a fetching lass, if I do say so. I fed her a big juicy beefsteak and she put it away so quick that I fed her another. That young lady can eat."

"It was generous of you," Uncle Seth said. "If I hadn't just et I'd have a beefsteak myself."

"What *was* the trouble?" Mr. Hickok inquired.

"Oh, Baldy Stone borrowed all our mules, and the girls thought he was stealing them. Then Mary Margaret shot Baldy's horse. At the time she was under the impression that the horse was an elk."

The part about the elk, which struck me as so curious, didn't seem to interest Wild Bill Hickok at all.

"Now why would Baldy Stone need to borrow a passel of mules?" he asked.

"He was hoping that good mounts would attract a posse," Uncle Seth said. "I believe he has had about enough of Jake Miller and that bunch over at Stumptown."

"Well, I don't agree with his thinking," Wild Bill said. "You can get shot just as dead off a good horse as off a bad horse. The quality of the posse is more important than the quality of the horses. How many posse men does he have signed up?"

"One, himself," Uncle Seth said.

"It would take a gallant fellow to ride off alone to tackle the Millers," Wild Bill said. "I haven't noticed that Baldy is that gallant."

After that there was a silence. Wild Bill seemed to be thinking about something. The bartender came over with a whiskey bottle and two glasses. Uncle Seth accepted a shot of whiskey, but waved off the second glass.

"This youth don't drink," he said. "But I do. You might just leave that bottle—that way you won't have to be traipsing back and forth. It'll give the dust a chance to settle."

Uncle Seth had spoken politely, something he didn't always bother to do, but the bartender, who was a feisty little fellow with a scar just under his lip, took offense at the remark.

"There's not a speck of dust on this floor," the bartender said. "What do you think I do all day and most of the night?"

"Just leave the bottle—there's no need for a dispute," Uncle Seth said.

"What does he think I do all day and most of the night?" the bartender asked Mr. Hickok, who didn't reply. The floor of the saloon had so many cigar butts strewn on it that it would have been hard to find much dust, but there was a pretty good pile of mud just inside the door where several mule skinners had scraped off their boots.

"That man has been working too hard—it's made him touchy," Uncle Seth said. "I get touchy myself, when I'm overworked."

"Let's hear more about this expedition to arrest the Millers," Mr. Hickok said. "The Millers have never disturbed me personally, but that goddamn Little Billy Perkins, who runs with them, has done me several bad turns."

"Little Billy has few morals—few to none," Uncle Seth said.

"He won't need morals, if he crosses me again," Mr. Hickok said. "It would be doing a favor to humanity to dispose of Little Billy, and I'm in the mood to do the favor.

"If the pay is decent, that is," he added.

He finished his little cigar and flipped the butt across the room. Then he pulled three more slim cigars out of his shirt pocket and offered one to Uncle Seth and one to me. He was a very polite man.

"This boy don't smoke, either," Uncle Seth said. "Mary Margaret is determined to raise him Christian."

"I doubt it will take," Mr. Hickok said, smiling at me. He lit his new cigar and tilted his chair back again.

"I believe Sheriff Stone is prepared to offer you

fifty dollars for your services, Bill," Uncle Seth said. "He only offered me five dollars, a sum I looked askance at."

Wild Bill Hickok laughed heartily at that piece of information. He seemed so relaxed and so friendly that I couldn't figure out why Uncle Seth had seemed nervous about going to see him. Behind us, the men in the front of the saloon didn't seem relaxed at all. Several of them were still glaring at us, a fact both Mr. Hickok and Uncle Seth continued to ignore.

"I wouldn't expect you to enjoy being offered forty-five dollars less than me, if I've got my subtraction right," Mr. Hickok said.

"You're accurate, both as to the sum and the opinion," Uncle Seth said.

Mr. Hickok blew a smoke ring or two and looked thoughtful.

"If they paid us fifty dollars apiece that would be a hundred dollars," he said. "I doubt the town has it. Do you suppose there's a rich citizen they could ask for a loan?"

"Well, Rosie McGee," Uncle Seth said.

I perked my ears up at that. Rosie McGee lived over the saloon. Once or twice I caught a glimpse of her, fanning herself in front of her window on sultry days. G.T. must have had a few glimpses, too, because Rosie was the woman he wanted to marry.

"I recall that Rosie harbors a grudge against Jake Miller," Uncle Seth said. "If she's still harboring her grudge she might be willing to make the community a loan.

"That's the best outlook," Uncle Seth went on. "If the town hired you, and Rosie hired me, we wouldn't have to put up with some ignorant posse men who would probably just be in the way."

Mr. Hickok blew another smoke ring.

"I don't know Miss McGee very well," he said. "It's possible that she harbors a grudge against me, too."

"She could even harbor a grudge against the town of Boone's Lick, in which case she might not care to contribute a cent," Uncle Seth speculated.

"Seth, it's time I tried to scare up a card game," Mr. Hickok said. "I can't just idle the night away discussing grudges—there's such a passel of them. But I'll contribute my services to this Stumptown expedition for fifty dollars—you'll have to scare up your own wages. I'm available anytime but Friday."

"Why not Friday?" Uncle Seth asked, as he got up from the table.

"I don't work Fridays—it's a firm rule," Mr. Hickok said. "Nice to meet you, Sherman."

"You see, he's superstitious," Uncle Seth said, as we were leaving the saloon. "All these fine gun-fighters have their superstitions."

There was a flight of stairs outside the saloon, going up to the room where Rosie McGee lived. Just as we were passing the steps I looked up and saw a little red glow at the top of the stairs—somebody was sitting on the landing, smoking a cigar. A cloud had crossed the moon—all I saw was a little glowing tip.

Uncle Seth saw it too. He took a step or two, and stopped.

"Shay, you go on home," he said. "I believe that's Rosie with the cheroot. I think I'll sound her out about the state of her grudges.

"Look out for Granpa," he added. "He might still be hunting that panther."

Then he turned back, and I soon heard him going up the stairs beside the saloon. The abrupt way he left me on my own gave me a lonely feeling, for some reason. It wasn't the dark—I walked around in the dark all the time, sometimes with G.T. and sometimes without him. I had enjoyed my visit with Wild Bill Hickok, but now I felt lonely. What I wished was that I could be grown-up, like Uncle Seth—grown-up enough to stop and talk with a woman bold enough to sit and smoke a cigar, at the top of the stairs, outside a saloon.

**6** W H E N  I got home Ma was in the graveyard. I was feeling a little better by then—it was a pretty night and I had walked off the loneliness. There was no sign of Granpa and his pistol but as I was passing the graveyard I saw Ma sitting on a little wooden bench, by the graves. One of Ma's sisters was buried there, and Granma Crackenthorpe, and my four little brothers who hadn't made it through the winters. There were some pretty bad winters in Missouri, and our cabin wasn't chinked too good. G.T. nearly died himself once, but with the help of an old woman who knew about poultices, he pulled through.

Ma had little Marcy with her—the baby was snoring in the quiet way little babies snore.

Sometimes I would get a knot in my throat when I came upon Ma sitting in the graveyard. I don't think a person would sit in a graveyard unless they were sad, and I didn't want to think about Ma being sad.

But there she was, not saying a thing, just sitting on her little bench, amid the graves.

"Hi, Ma," I said.

She looked behind me.

"Seth didn't come back with you?" she asked.

"I think he wanted to play cards," I said.

Ma motioned for me to sit down beside her on the bench, something she rarely did. When Ma went to the graveyard she usually made it clear that she wanted to be left alone.

"Don't be lying for him, Shay," she said. "Let him lie for himself, if there has to be a lie."

I didn't know what to say to that. I didn't even know why I lied—it just came out. I don't know whether Ma cared or not, what Uncle Seth did with Rosie McGee.

It seemed to me the best thing to do would be to change the subject, to something I felt sure would get Ma's attention.

"Uncle Seth wants to take G.T. and me with the posse," I said. "The sheriff's getting up a posse to go arrest the Millers, over at Stumptown, and Uncle Seth thinks me and G.T. are old enough to go along."

"Did you hear me, Shay?" Ma asked, ignoring my statement completely. "I said don't lie for your Uncle Seth—and don't lie for your Pa, either, if he ever comes home again. Let grown men do their own lying—I mean it."

"Yes ma'am," I said meekly. "I'm sorry. I don't know why I said it."

Then Ma put her head in her hands and cried. The baby woke up and began to cry too. I didn't know what to do, but I didn't dare leave the bench. I put my arm around Ma, but she kept crying. I knew that when Ma went out to the graveyard at night she went there to do her crying. We all knew that, and took care to give the graveyard a wide berth, if Ma was in it. But this time I had been careless and here I was. Ma cried and the baby cried—I felt for a minute like I might cry too, although I didn't know of anything I needed to cry about. Mainly I just wished Uncle Seth would show up. He was the one person who could get Ma feeling better, when she was low.

It felt like Ma was going to cry forever, but I guess it wasn't forever. She stopped crying and then the baby stopped. Once they were both calmed down, Ma let Marcy nurse a little.

"I'm glad you didn't leave, Shay," Ma said, when she was herself again. "The ability to stay put when a woman's crying is not one most men have.

"You're fifteen," she added. "I expect you'll soon have a woman of your own. Take my advice and just stay put when she cries. You don't have to say anything: just don't leave. If you can just keep your seat until the crying's over it'll be better for both of you."

I had no comment on that. At the moment I didn't expect I'd ever have a woman of my own—I probably wouldn't need to worry about the crying part.

"I guess your uncle ran into Rosie," Ma said.

I didn't answer, so she gave me a little poke in the ribs with her elbow.

"Mind your manners," Ma said. "Answer me when I ask a question."

"He was going to try and see if she'd pay him fifty dollars to go with the posse," I said. I didn't think Uncle Seth would mind if I told that much.

"What? Say that again?" Ma asked, so I said it again.

"You're just a babe in the woods, Shay," Ma said. Then she chuckled, kind of deep in her throat.

"Rosie don't pay men fifty dollars," Ma said. "It's the other way around—men pay Rosie fifty dollars. Maybe a little less, maybe a little more, depending. But Rosie don't pay men."

I had thought the notion that Rosie McGee would chip in fifty dollars to send Uncle Seth with the posse was a little far-fetched, myself. If the sheriff was only willing to pay him five dollars to go shoot at the Miller gang, why would Rosie McGee want to pay him fifty dollars to do the same job? Of course, the fifty dollars only came up because that was what the sheriff offered to pay Wild Bill Hickok. It seemed like a world of money to me.

"What was she supposed to pay Seth the fifty dollars *for*?" Ma asked. She seemed a lot more cheerful now that we had started talking about Uncle Seth. Even without being there, he was helping to cheer Ma up.

"He seemed to think she'd want him to catch Jake Miller," I said. "That's what he and Mr. Hickok were talking about. Uncle Seth wants to take me and G.T. along with the posse when they go to Stumptown."

"I heard you slip that in the first time," Ma said. Marcy was wide awake—she had been trying to crawl lately. Ma put her down on the ground on her belly, to see if she was making any progress with her crawling. Marcy hadn't made much. She just waved her arms and grunted.

"You can do it!" Ma said, to encourage her. "Get up on your hands and legs and crawl."

Marcy continued to wave her arms and legs and grunt.

"She'll figure it out in a few more days," Ma said. She left Marcy to struggle with the problem.

"Your Uncle Seth don't know anything about women," Ma said, looking at me. "He's God's fool, where women are concerned. Rosie McGee won't give him a cent, although it is a fact that she hates Jake Miller."

"Why?" I asked.

She didn't answer, which meant that in her opinion, why wasn't any of my business.

"Can we go with the posse, then?" I asked. I was excited at that prospect, but Ma had been so careful about us during the wartime that I didn't know if there was much hope.

"If Seth wants to take you, you can go," Ma said. "But I can't bear to lose no more boys, so you've got to promise to look after G.T."

I expected her to tell me to be careful and look

after myself—when she only asked me to look after G.T. I got my feelings hurt, for a moment. G.T. had always been an expert at looking after himself. Didn't Ma care about me?

"You're the mature one," Ma said, as if in answer to the question I hadn't asked. "Seth don't know anything about women but otherwise he can take care of himself. But G.T. don't know anything about anything, and besides that he's reckless. You make sure he don't get hurt."

"I'll do my best, but he don't mind me," I reminded her.

Ma looked at me a long time, then.

"Here's a piece of news for you, Shay," she said. "The reason I'm letting you boys go with the posse is because you're going to need a little exposure to the wild side of things."

I didn't know what to say.

"I've got some news for you all," Ma said. "I'm tired of sitting here in Missouri, going hungry and losing weight. When we finish eating this horse I shot, we're going to take a trip—all of us."

That was startling news. The bunch of us had always lived in the same place. G.T. and me had only been up and down the river a town or two from Boone's Lick, and the towns weren't very far apart. Other than that we had always just lived in the cabin near the river.

"Where will we go?" I asked.

"To wherever your pa is," Ma said. "I'm out of patience with him. This baby's about ready to crawl and he's never laid eyes on her. He's not been home in fourteen months, and then it was only for two nights. If he won't come and see us, then we'll go and see him. And if he don't like it I'll leave him."

Then she scooped up Marcy and headed for the cabin, leaving me where I sat, with thoughts buzzing around in my head like bumblebees. Just the fact that Ma was going to allow us to go off with the posse would have been enough to think about, but on top of that came the news about a trip to see Pa, wherever he was. Once the fact of it sunk in a little I got so excited I wanted to run around in circles. I wanted to wake up G.T. and tell him the double good news, about the posse and the trip, but it turned out I didn't have to wake him up. Just as I was trying to think of some way to work off my excitement, G.T. came walking up from the river, carrying a dead coon by the tail.

"I slipped up on him while he was cracking a mussel," G.T. said. "Coon meat's just as good as horse meat—there just ain't as much of it."

I was dying to spill my news but I knew I had better take a minute to admire G.T.'s kill, or he'd pout for a week.

"What'd you do, chunk it?" I asked.

"Chunked it," G.T. said.

"Guess what, we're going on a trip—two trips, that is," I said, unable to hold the news a minute longer. "First we're going with the posse, and then we're going upriver to look for Pa."

"You're lying!" G.T. said. Then he stomped off in a sulk, because I hadn't paid enough attention to his coon.

**7** G.T. and I had a fistfight—a short one—before the night was over. I crawled up in the loft of the cabin, where we kids slept, and was trying to calm down and get some sleep when G.T. shot up the ladder and started punching me. That was the way G.T. started all his fights—he was a firm believer in getting in the first lick. He got in about three licks and I managed two before Neva woke up and yelled at us. Ma heard Neva and got into it right away.

"G.T., do you want me to come up there?" Ma asked.

G.T. definitely didn't, so that was the end of that fight.

"I'll beat the stuffings out of you tomorrow," he whispered, before settling down to snore.

It was only then that I remembered that Ma had

said she would leave Pa, if he didn't welcome our visit—that was an unsettling thought, for sure.

It seemed like only a few minutes later that the racket started in the freight yard. When Uncle Seth shook me awake the world was white, with a close, chilly mist off the river.

"Bring your brother," Uncle Seth said, which was easier said than done. G.T. was a sound sleeper. I shook him and shook him—finally Neva stuck a pin in his toe, two or three times, which brought him around. We could hear horses in the freight yard—or maybe they were our mules. Ma gave us chickory coffee, a rare treat.

"You need to get your wits stirring, if you're going off with these long riders here," she said.

The only long rider I could see, besides Uncle Seth, was Sheriff Baldy Stone, who was evidently cold natured. He stood by the fireplace, warming his hands.

"Eddie, it's just eight miles to Stumptown," Ma said. "What's the point of leaving so early?"

"The point is, there might be a siege," the sheriff said, "and if it's a long siege we stand to leave the services of Mr. Hickok. This is Thursday and he don't work on Fridays. I want to take advantage of as much of Thursday as I can."

"There's another thing," Ma said. "I've told Seth and I'll tell you and I'll even tell Mr. Hickok, if he puts in an appearance."

"What's the other thing?" the sheriff asked.

"I expect you to bring both my boys back alive, that's the other thing," Ma said.

Then she gave us a few strips of horse meat to

stuff in our saddlebags, after which she went outside and disappeared in the mist.

"You heard her, now stay alive," the sheriff said. "I would rather not be on the bad side of your ma."

"For that matter, I'd rather not be dead," I remarked. G.T., who was still half asleep, thought it was so funny that he cackled—even Neva giggled.

When we went out to the lots we found that Uncle Seth had already saddled each of us a mule, and Mr. Hickok *was* there, sitting off to himself on a good sorrel horse. Ma was just walking away from him when we came out. I imagine she was warning him, just as she had warned the sheriff.

She didn't say another word to us, which upset G.T. a little.

"I hope she don't forget to skin my coon," he said—his lower lip was trembling. I doubt it was really that coon that he had on his mind.

Uncle Seth seemed to be in a quiet mood, which was unusual for him. Everybody had rifles *and* pistols except us, which didn't sit well with G.T.

"I need a pistol and so does Shay," he said.

"No, no side arms for you boys," Uncle Seth said. "Side arms are only reliable in the hands of experts, and sometimes not then. I'm not too comfortable with the notion of Baldy having a pistol, but it's too early in the day to be disarming the sheriff. Is that your opinion, Bill?"

"I am rarely up this early," Mr. Hickok said. "I don't have an opinion."

"I've put you boys on the fastest mules," Uncle Seth said. "That way you can outrun the Millers if you have to."

Mr. Hickok was all wrapped up in a gray slicker. He took one hand out from under his slicker and pointed his finger several times.

"Shooting a pistol is just a matter of pointing," he said. "If you can point straight you can shoot straight.

"Very few people can point straight," he added, and then he didn't say another word until we were almost to Stumptown.

It was the thickest mist, that morning. If there hadn't been a well-marked track between Boone's Lick and Stumptown I have no doubt we would all have got lost from one another. Some of the time I couldn't even see my mule's head. I had to listen for the jingling of the bits and the creaking of the saddle leather to convince myself that I was still with the group. Sometimes the mist would clear for a minute and I would see everybody plain as day, but then it would close in again, white as cotton, and I'd have to proceed on hearing.

G.T. was bothered by the ground mist, too. He was so anxious not to lose me that he kept bumping my mule, Little Nicky, a mule with a tendency to bite when he got irritated.

"You best quit bumping Nicky," I told G.T. "He'll take a bite out of you, if you're not careful."

"If he bites me I'll shoot him," G.T. said. "It's spooky out here. I wish I'd stayed home and butchered my coon."

"Well, you didn't," I pointed out.

"I'd go back, if I could find my way," G.T. said. "If you'd go with me I expect we could both make it back."

"Hush, G.T.," Uncle Seth said. "We're trying to take the Millers by surprise, which we won't do if you keep chattering."

"That's right, button up," Sheriff Baldy said.

There was no more talk from G.T. but I knew he was resentful—he never liked being scolded.

Myself, I was feeling queasy in my stomach, even though I'd had no vittles except Ma's chickory coffee. I felt like I usually felt when Uncle Seth took us bear hunting. We saw no bears on any of the hunts but of course a bear can appear at any time.

"They like to spring at you from hiding," Uncle Seth said cheerfully, and all day, that's what I kept expecting would happen. A bear would spring at us from hiding.

The prospect worried G.T. too.

"How many shots does it take to kill a bear?" he asked Uncle Seth, several times. G.T. had a habit of repeating his questions over and over again. Uncle Seth told him that the number of shots depended on where the bear was hit but the explanation wasn't thorough enough for G.T. What he wanted was a clear notion of how many times he'd have to shoot a bear, if one sprang out at him from hiding.

Uncle Seth finally lost his temper.

"How many licks of a hammer would it take to make you shut up, you hardheaded fool?" he asked G.T.

"I just wish the dern bear would spring out, if it's going to," G.T. said.

I felt the same way about the men we were going

to attack. I wanted the Millers to spring out, if they were going to, so I'd know whether my fate was to be alive or dead. All three of the older men had strict instructions from Ma to see that we got back alive, but of course, in the heat of battle they would have to look out for themselves first. There were no guarantees—or so few that I was still a little shocked that Ma had let us go. I guess she figured it was time we grew up and learned to fight, in case there was fighting to be done on the trip we would be making shortly, once the Stumptown business was over with.

All the same, things were happening too quickly. Only yesterday I had been a boy, with nothing on my mind except watching my brother fish for crawdads, or my uncle shoot the heads off turtles. When the sun was going down I was peacefully helping my mother cut up a dead horse; now the sun was just rising—it had begun to burn away the mist, turning patches of it a golden color—and here I was an armed man, riding off with other armed men, to kill or be killed.

"I am pleased to see there's going to be a fine sunlight today," Uncle Seth said.

"That may be, Seth," the sheriff said, "but there's something I *ain't* pleased to see: the dern Tebbits."

He pointed toward two men in black coats, just visible through the drifting mist. They were sitting their skinny horses right in the path.

"Now, Sheriff, reinforcements can't hurt," Uncle Seth said. "The Millers might be having a family reunion or something, in which case a little more firepower would be to our advantage."

Mr. Hickok glanced at the two men in black coats, but made no comment.

"What's the matter, Baldy?" Uncle Seth asked, lowering his voice. "Is it that you think they mean to rob us—or do you just doubt their allegiance?"

"Both," Sheriff Baldy said. "Hush up, Seth."

The Tebbits, if that was who they were, didn't offer to move out of the path, when we came close.

"Hello, Newt—hello, Percy," the sheriff said. "It's strange to come upon you this early. I suppose you spent the night in the road."

"You're on the move early yourself, Sheriff," the one called Newt remarked. "Going worming, are you?"

"We're on official business," the sheriff replied. "It don't do to lie abed when there's official business to be conducted."

"We want to join the posse," the one called Percy informed him.

"There's no need, we're fully staffed," the sheriff said.

Both Tebbits gave ugly snorts at that reply.

"Two Yankees and two boys and you, that's all I see," Newt Tebbit said. "That's not enough."

"They've got our sister Nancy," Percy Tebbit said. "We fear that dern Ronnie Miller may have led her astray."

"You wouldn't deny two brothers the chance to rescue their sister from a swamp of sin, would you?" Newt Tebbit asked.

It was clear that the Tebbits had managed to put Sheriff Baldy on the spot. He looked at Mr. Hickok and he looked at Uncle Seth, but both of them were just waiting politely, with faraway looks in their eyes. If either of them had even noticed the Tebbits they gave no sign.

I believe the sheriff decided there was no way around taking the two men, not unless he wanted to provoke a gunfight before we even got to the main battle.

"If that's the situation, of course you can come," he said. "But I've no money to pay you for your time. How are you fixed for ammunition?"

"We've got enough cartridges, I guess," Newt Tebbit said. "You needn't be concerned about the pay. We'll see what we can pick up once we rout the killers."

"Fall in, then," the sheriff said.

**8** P R E T T Y soon the mist burned off completely and we rode on to Stumptown through as pretty a morning as you'd want. It was the sort of warm bright day that usually put Uncle Seth in a high good humor. Sometimes he whistled on such days, or even sang a ditty or two—"Buffalo Gals," or something he'd learned on the river. At the very least he might tease G.T. by making up riddles that G.T. couldn't possibly guess the answer to.

This morning, though, the fine sunshine seemed to have no effect on him. He was lost in thought again; and Mr. Hickok was no jollier than Uncle Seth. Maybe that was because they knew we were headed for a dangerous fight. But then bear hunting was a dangerous proceeding and bear hunting had never dampened Uncle Seth's spirits, that I could remember.

Stumptown was not a large community—in fact, so far as being a town went, it only had two buildings, a store and a church. When we got in sight of it we stopped on a little ridge to look it over. There were a few crab apple trees on the ridge, with several crab apples scattered on the ground nearby.

"A bear has been picking over those crab apples," Uncle Seth observed.

Nobody had any answer to that.

There was no sign of life in Stumptown. I saw a rooster, walking around on the porch of the store, but that was it.

"It's just a mile to the Millers'," Sheriff Baldy said. "They live south of the village."

We all started to move down the ridge toward the two buildings, but the Tebbit brothers didn't move with us. Just the way they sat on their horses looking at us made me uneasy—I have no explanation for the feeling. The Tebbits didn't seem friendly— not even to one another.

"What's wrong, boys?" the sheriff asked, when he saw that the Tebbit brothers hadn't moved off the ridge.

"We'd best give that town a wide berth—be a perfect place for an ambush," Newt Tebbit said. "There's some brushy thickets off to the east. I say we slip around that way."

"Why wouldn't a brushy thicket be just as good a place for an ambush as a little two-building town?" Uncle Seth asked.

"I second the question," Mr. Hickok said.

"I agree with my brother," Percy Tebbit said. "A swing to the east would be the safe way to go."

"Who lives in Stumptown, besides Old Lady Mobley?" Sheriff Baldy asked.

"Nobody—just Old Lady Mobley—but that don't mean the Miller gang couldn't slip in and hide in the church," Newt Tebbit argued.

"I didn't send them no telegram, informing them of our arrival," the sheriff said. "They have no reason to hide in the church—or anywhere else."

"News gets around," Percy Tebbit said.

"This palaver is a waste of time—remember that I don't work on Fridays," Mr. Hickok said.

He turned his horse, and so did Uncle Seth. The two of them rode up on the Tebbits, who held their ground.

"Ain't we missing a Tebbit?" Uncle Seth asked. "I had in mind that there was three of you Tebbits, not counting your womenfolk."

"That's right, there's Charlie," Sheriff Baldy said. "Why didn't Charlie come? Doesn't he want to save his own sister?"

"Charlie had a toothache," Newt Tebbit said calmly. "He's gone to Boone's Lick to locate a dentist. We expect him to be along once he gets that tooth out."

I was getting a feeling that something was about to happen, on the ridge. Uncle Seth and Mr. Hickok were walking their horses real slow, toward the Tebbits. Sheriff Baldy was chewing on an unlit cigar. There was a feeling of waiting. Uncle Seth had told us about the war, when bombs and cannons were always going off. He said there was a certain feeling men got just before a battle that was like no other feeling. "You're waiting, and you don't know what you're waiting for," he said. "You just know it won't be good, and it might even be death."

That was how I felt as Uncle Seth and Mr. Hickok closed with the Tebbits. Both Tebbits bared their teeth as Uncle Seth and Mr. Hickok rode toward them. I wondered why they were grinning, although it was more like they were snarling, as a badger snarls, or a ferret.

"I don't know about his tooth, but I suspect Charlie Tebbit's the one hiding in that brushy thicket you mentioned," Uncle Seth said.

"You are goddamn brash, Seth Cecil," Newt Tebbit said, but before he could continue his speech Uncle Seth swung his Sharps rifle and knocked the man off his horse.

"I hope it won't be necessary for me to hit you that hard," Mr. Hickok said to Percy Tebbit. He had slipped a pistol out from under his gray slicker, and was pointing it at Percy. While Percy was staring at Mr. Hickok, trying to decide what to do, Uncle Seth came up on his blind side and whacked him too. Percy Tebbit slid off his horse slowly, like a sack of oats slides off a pile.

"You might have damaged your pistol, if *you'd* slugged him," Uncle Seth said. "A side arm is not supposed to be used as a hammer."

Both of the Tebbits were down but neither one of them was out. They were writhing around on the ground, holding their heads. Percy was bleeding profusely, but Newt didn't seem to be cut. Sheriff Baldy rode over and looked down at them.

"Goddamn the luck," he said. "This is just the sort of complication I wanted to avoid."

"Yes . . . and Thursday's slipping away," Mr. Hickok said.

"I hope you brought some handcuffs—it will eliminate the need for tying knots," Uncle Seth said.

"I did, six pair," the sheriff said, pulling a tangle of handcuffs out of his saddlebag. "I didn't expect to have to waste any on the Tebbits though."

"If I were you I'd handcuff them while they're still groggy," Mr. Hickok advised. "It wouldn't surprise me if they showed some fight."

The sheriff jumped down and got to it. He had just clicked the cuffs on the two men when both of them began to yell.

"Come, boys! Come, boys!" they yelled, as loud as they could. Then they both staggered up and began to run down the ridge, at which point seven or eight men, all mounted, burst out of one of the thickets east of Stumptown.

"Well, there's your ambush," Uncle Seth said matter-of-factly. "What do you say, Bill? Should we make a run for the church? The cover is sparse on this hill."

"I count eight riders," Mr. Hickok said, getting off his horse. "We are five. That only gives them an advantage of three. Look at them flail their nags! I doubt that any of them can shoot straight from a running horse, and besides that, those puny horses will give out long before they get here. Let's not disturb ourselves any more than is necessary."

We all dismounted and watched the ambushers, who were still quite a long distance away. Uncle Seth took the oilcloth off his rifle. He had a little tripod which he sometimes set up for long-distance shooting—he could rest his rifle barrel on it if he needed to take a fine sight.

"Which one am I supposed to shoot?" G.T. asked. Sheriff Baldy and Mr. Hickok were calmly watching the ambushers come. I wasn't calm, myself—I wanted to start shooting right away, but like G.T., I wasn't sure who I was supposed to shoot at.

"Wait, boys—they're out of range," Uncle Seth said. "I'll shoot a horse or two, and when I do you count to ten before you fire—that goes for you too, G.T."

"Shoot a horse or two, Seth—it might discourage them," Mr. Hickok said.

"How far will this rifle shoot?" G.T. asked. "Somebody tell me, quick."

I didn't blame G.T. for asking the question. I had no idea how far my own rifle would shoot. I had killed two deer with it, and several wild pigs and a wolf, but none of those critters had been very far away, and I think the old wolf must have been sick, otherwise he would never have let me get as close as I did. I couldn't keep a clear focus on the men who were charging toward us—one minute they looked as big as giants, and the next minute they looked tiny—so tiny I knew I'd be lucky to hit one of them without using up a lot of ammunition. Uncle Seth had given me ten cartridges, and G.T. the same.

Nobody answered G.T. Uncle Seth had set up his tripod, but he hadn't drawn a bead yet. Mr. Hickok and the sheriff were as cool as if they were watching the Fourth of July parade.

"I see Jake Miller, and I believe that's Ronnie just behind him," the sheriff said. "We might land the whole family in the next few minutes."

Mr. Hickok was not so optimistic.

"There's no sign of Billy Perkins, though," he said. "I wouldn't expect him to be as foolish as these men, charging up a hill at five riflemen. It would occur to Billy Perkins that one or two of the riflemen might be competent shots."

Then Uncle Seth laid his rifle across his little tripod and proved Mr. Hickok's point. Before G.T. and I could get our wits together and start counting, Uncle Seth shot twice and brought down two horses—their riders went sprawling off into the grass.

"Drop one more, why don't you, Seth?" Mr. Hickok suggested. "The loss of one more horse might bring them to their senses."

"I was wrong, that ain't Jake Miller—it's just his cousin Eli," Sheriff Baldy said. "They favor one another quite a bit."

Uncle Seth fired again and a third horse went

down—though just saying it went down would be to put it too mildly. The third horse turned a complete somersault. Its rider flew off about thirty feet, after which he didn't move.

"It's rare to see a horse turn a flip like that," Uncle Seth observed.

"That was Ronnie Miller's horse," Sheriff Baldy said. "Ronnie took a hard fall. He ain't moving."

The two Tebbit brothers, both still handcuffed, stopped about halfway between us and the riders. Then the riders stopped too, all except one, who came on about another fifty yards before it dawned on him that he was no longer part of a group, after which he quickly drew rein.

"That's Charlie Tebbit out in front," the sheriff said. "I knew that story about the toothache was a damn lie."

"Do you see anyone you particularly want to shoot, Seth?" Mr. Hickok asked.

"No, not if they're cowed—I've seen too much war to wantonly spill blood," Uncle Seth said.

"Let's keep our guns cocked," Mr. Hickok suggested. "They may not be quite cowed."

I didn't know whether the ambushers were cowed or not, but I was happy they had called off their charge. I had started my count and was up to six when the lead rider pulled rein.

"Stop counting, G.T., we don't need to shoot," I said. Once G.T. started something, it was hard to get him stopped. I saw his lips moving, so I figured he was still counting—then his rifle clicked, indicating that I had been right.

"Uh-oh, forgot to load," he said.

"Well, load then, but don't shoot," I said.

"I'm reasonably pleased with my shooting," Uncle Seth said. "The tripod is a fine invention."

The Tebbit brothers weren't pleased with anything, though. The fact that the ambushers had pulled up annoyed them greatly.

"Charlie, come get us!" Newt yelled. "Why'd you stop?"

"Why does he think they stopped?" Mr. Hickok said, amused. He lit one of his thin cigars. "Seth was shooting all their horses—that's why they stopped."

"It's our play, Baldy—what do you want to do?" Uncle Seth asked.

"I'm not sure," Sheriff Baldy said.

"Thursday's slipping away," Mr. Hickok reminded him, though it was still early enough that the morning mist had just burned off.

**9** I GUESS from the sheriff's point of view the situation must have looked complicated. The ambushers were sort of milling around, paying no attention at all to Newt and Percy Tebbit, who were still hoping to be rescued. Two of the men who had been spilled off their horses were back on their feet, but they weren't walking too steady. Ronnie Miller, the man whose horse had turned a flip, wasn't moving at all.

"Do you suppose this bunch would agree to be arrested?" the sheriff asked. "It's a passel of people to cram into jail, much less feed."

"Arrested for what?" Uncle Seth asked. "All they did was race their horses—you can't arrest people for holding horse races."

Mr. Hickok raised an eyebrow at Uncle Seth's remark, but the sheriff just looked confused.

"What?" he asked.

"So far I'm the only one who's broken the law," Uncle Seth went on. "I just shot three horses that didn't belong to me, and I may have killed that fellow whose horse flipped over."

"No, I seen him stir," Mr. Hickok said. "I expect him to get up any minute."

The sheriff looked even more confused. It was the kind of thing Uncle Seth was always doing: turning some simple matter around so that everybody became confused. I've heard Ma flare up at him a hundred times, for just that sort of thing.

"How can you say that to me, Seth! Why would you say such a thing to me?" Ma would say. Sometimes she'd cry and sometimes there'd be bitter words—Uncle Seth would always just sit there with a pleasant look on his face, until the storm blew over.

"There's nothing wrong with looking at the other fellow's point of view," he might say, if he said anything.

"Yes there *is*!" Ma would cry. "Yes, there is. Just look at *my* point of view! That's what you need to worry about."

The ambushers were still milling around. It was clear that they couldn't decide what to do. The two Tebbits had yelled themselves hoarse, but nobody seemed interested in rescuing them. Finally they began to hobble on down the slope, as fast as they could hobble. The man whose horse had flipped got up on his hands and knees.

"Ronnie Miller must be lucky," Uncle Seth said. "A tumble like that could easily have broken his neck."

"This would be a simpler situation if the two men we really want were here," Mr. Hickok said. "That would be Jake Miller and Little Billy Perkins."

"And Cut-Nose," the sheriff said. "Cut-Nose is a pretty cold killer."

"As to that I wouldn't know," Mr. Hickok said. "All I see are a bunch of amateur ambushers. If they knew their business they would have fallen on us while we were still in the mist. Seth's tripod wouldn't have been much use in that mist."

About that time the two Tebbits finally reached the gang of horsemen. Though all the horses were skinny, the Tebbits and the men whose horses Uncle Seth had shot climbed up behind the mounted men; then they all rode away. Some of the puny little horses could barely stagger along, under the weight of two men and their saddles and gear.

"Damnit, this is awkward—they're headed for the Miller shack," Sheriff Baldy said.

"It's worse than awkward—something ain't right," Uncle Seth said. "That was too easy, even if I *am* good at shooting horses out from under people."

"Agreed—I believe they've flanked us," Mr. Hickok said. "The *real* team, I mean."

Uncle Seth and Mr. Hickok began to amble around as if the departure of the ambushers had confused them so badly that they didn't know which way to turn. In the course of their ambling both of them switched from the uphill to the downhill side of their horses.

"Don't look, boys," Uncle Seth said. "Baldy, you're likely to be the first man shot unless you change your position and change it quick."

"I don't think anybody's behind—" the sheriff said, before a bullet splatted into him and knocked him off his horse.

"Duck behind your horses, boys—do it quick," Uncle Seth said. G.T. and I were quick to obey.

The gang behind us wasn't as numerous as the gang in front of us—on the other hand, they were a lot closer. They were no more than two hundred yards away, and there were six of them that I could see.

"Do we still have to count to ten?" I asked Uncle Seth, but I never got an answer: he was too busy shooting, and so was Mr. Hickok and Sheriff Baldy, who didn't seem to be dead.

"These Rebs, they love a cavalry charge," Uncle Seth commented, at one point. Just then I heard G.T.'s teeth chattering—his teeth always went to clacking when he was nervous or scared, whether it was a cold day or not.

"By God, they've flushed that bear you mentioned, Seth," Sheriff Baldy said—and it was the truth. The new bunch of ambushers had run right up on a large black bear that must have been taking a nap behind a rock. He woke up from his nap to find himself in the midst of a gun battle, which he didn't want any part of. The ambushers were nearly on top of the bear before any of them saw him—they were too busy shooting at us. The sight of a bear square in their way startled them a good deal, and did worse than startle their horses, most of which flew into wild buckings.

"Hold your fire," Uncle Seth said. "Baldy, you need to deputize that bear—he's doing our work better than we could do it."

That was easy to see. The bear ran through the horses and the horses went wild. Pretty soon riders were flying off in every direction—the horses, once shut of their riders, went tearing off toward Stumptown. Only one of the six riders managed to keep his seat.

"That's Little Billy Perkins. Hands off," Mr. Hickok said, pointing at the one man who was still in the saddle. Mr. Hickok jumped on his horse— Little Billy Perkins spotted him at once and took off down the slope. He was mounted on a long-legged bay—soon they were nearly flying. Mr. Hickok tried to cut him off but his sorrel wasn't fast enough—the bay had the lead and was widening it by the minute as the two riders headed for the distant trees.

"That's the horse you should have shot, Seth," Sheriff Baldy said.

"Too late now," Uncle Seth said. "Wild Bill may have to break his Friday rule if he hopes to catch that fellow."

"What about the bear—I don't see him," G.T. said.

"No, he probably went home," Uncle Seth said.

"I don't think he appreciated having his nap interrupted."

"I expect he's hiding somewhere, waiting to spring out," G.T. said. That was my opinion too, although I didn't say it.

"Oh no, Mr. Bear won't be back today," Uncle Seth assured us. "We need to go arrest these killers. Baldy, are you hurt bad?"

"No, the bullet hit the back of my saddle before it hit me, which is a good thing," the sheriff said. "The ball fell out. I'm bloody but I ain't in danger."

"Then let's go handcuff this crew before they run off," Uncle Seth said.

"I see Jake Miller," the sheriff said. "He's squirming around as if he's hurt, but it could be a trick."

"If he ain't hurt, and it's a trick, then I'll hurt him," Uncle Seth said. "I resent being ambushed by a Reb who won't admit his side lost."

"We need to be careful, Seth," the sheriff said. "Cut-Nose is on his feet but he's favoring one ankle—I believe he lost his rifle in the fall."

"I'm always careful, Baldy," Uncle Seth said. "You supply the handcuffs—I'll supply the caution."

**10** Cut-Nose Jones seemed dazed—
he was under the impression that he was
in Ohio. He put up no fight when the
sheriff handcuffed him.

"His own horse kicked him in the head—I seen
it," Lester Miller said. "Them horses was in a
hurry to get away from that bear."

Two of the ambushers had hobbled off, but
Lester, a boy the same age as G.T., had stayed to
help his brother Jake, who had broken his leg in
the fall. Even with Uncle Seth pointing his rifle
right between the man's eyes the sheriff had a tussle getting him securely handcuffed. Jake Miller
hissed like a snake the whole time.

"Don't let him grab your gun—he's got fight in
him yet," Uncle Seth warned; but Sheriff Baldy,

despite being round as a barrel, was expert at hand-cuffing dangerous criminals: he gave Jake Miller a short sharp kick in his broken leg and got the cuffs on him while the man was yelling.

Lester Miller was no problem to handcuff—I think he was glad the fight was over.

"They gave me a poor gun," he said. "The hammer's just wired on, you see."

"I wasn't allowed much in the way of guns when I was your age," Uncle Seth said sociably.

"Shut up, you whimpering brat!" Jake Miller said—then he actually tried to butt his little brother with his head.

"Who were the men who ran away?" Sheriff Baldy asked.

"Jody and Lyle, I don't know their last names," Lester said.

With Jake Miller and Cut-Nose Jones safely handcuffed and disarmed, Uncle Seth got back on his horse and rode off toward Stumptown—some of the horses had run themselves out and were standing there looking tired. That left me and G.T. and the sheriff to watch the prisoners. Even though they were securely handcuffed and we had all the guns, I didn't feel particularly comfortable with this responsibility, and neither did G.T. Jake Miller was about as mad as a man can get—he looked at me with little hot eyes, the way a boar hog looks at you just before he charges. Just looking at him made me want to back up a step or two.

"You two Yankee boys have made a big mistake," he said.

"No, I have never made a mistake in my life," G.T. informed him. It was G.T.'s disputatious side coming out.

"Don't let him rattle you, boys," Sheriff Baldy said—for some reason his voice trailed off, when he said "boys."

When I looked around Sheriff Baldy was lying flat on his back on the ground—he had either died or slipped into a faint.

"He's dead—good," Jake Miller said matter-of-factly. "The son of a bitch was fatal shot and didn't know it. Now you Yankee boys get these handcuffs off me, if you want to live."

I looked down the hill, hoping Uncle Seth was on his way back. But he wasn't. The horse he was trying to catch was skittish, and wouldn't quite let himself be caught. Uncle Seth wasn't even looking our way, which meant that he didn't know Sheriff Baldy had fainted or died.

"You stay right where you are," I told Jake Miller. I tried to sound determined, like Ma would have sounded. But I wasn't Ma, and Jake Miller knew it.

"Do as I say, you damned Yankee pup," he said. "You pups had no business coming after me in the first place. Turn me loose or when I get out I'll track you to the ends of the earth and cut your throats."

"I guess he'd do it, too," Lester Miller said—he seemed a little shocked by his big brother's savage talk.

"We better shoot him, Shay," G.T. said. "He's got them mean eyes."

"No," I said. "What can he do? He's handcuffed and he's got a broken leg."

I had no more than said it than Jake Miller launched himself at me, somehow—made a wild lunge. Broken leg or no broken leg he managed to jump at me and grab my gun barrel. But I had my finger on the trigger and when Jake tried to yank my gun out of my hand the yank caused me to pull the trigger. The shot hit Jake right in the chest and knocked him back across Sheriff Baldy's body.

"Good shot," G.T. said.

"Uh-oh, Jake's kilt!" Lester Miller said. "That's going to make Ronnie and Tommy awful mad."

But Jake Miller wasn't kilt. His eyes were wide open and he was still mad. He even started to try and pull one of Sheriff Baldy's pistols out of its holster, but the sheriff came back to consciousness just in time to roll away from him.

"Help me, boys—drag me off, I'm faint," the sheriff said. G.T. and I caught his arms and tried to drag him well out of the way of Jake Miller, who was crawling after us, still hoping to grab a pistol, the fire of hatred in his eyes.

"Get back! How come you ain't kilt?" G.T. asked.

I would have liked an answer to that question too, since I had shot Jake point-blank, right in the chest. If that wasn't enough to kill a man, what did it take?

"You pups—I aim to cut your throats, and yours too, Baldy," Jake Miller said, and then he began to curse; but his cursing wasn't quite as vigorous as it had been when the sheriff was handcuffing him, so at least my bullet had taken a little bit of the ginger out of him.

Just then Uncle Seth loped up—he had finally caught the skittish horse.

"My goodness, can't nobody but me do anything right?" he asked.

He jumped down, grabbed Jake Miller by the hair, and slammed his head into the ground a time or two, real hard—it was enough to take the fight out of Jake, at least for a while.

"The sheriff fainted and while he was out Jake grabbed my rifle barrel and I shot him," I said, in a rush. "I don't know why he won't die."

"Because he don't want to, son," Uncle Seth said. "Folks are tougher than they look, and quite a few are unwilling to die unless they just can't get around it."

"But I shot him point-blank," I said. I was shocked that the man wasn't dead.

"So I see," Uncle Seth said, opening Jake Miller's shirt. There was a hole in his chest but not a very big one. Uncle Seth rolled him over and pulled up his shirt—there was a bigger hole in his back, where the bullet came out, but it still wasn't the size hole I was expecting to see.

"The bullet went right through—it didn't hit nothing vital," Uncle Seth said. "If you're going to make a habit of shooting at these surly outlaws, then you need to learn where their vitals are."

"What's a vital?" G.T. asked.

"Heart, lungs, stomach, gut," Uncle Seth said.

"If I had a tablet I could draw you a picture." Since he didn't have a tablet he rolled Jake Miller over on his back and proceeded to give us a quick lesson, pointing with his finger at the places we ought to aim for.

"Now, the heart's here, and the lungs here, and the stomach down here, and the liver and the kidneys kind of tucked around in this area," he said.

I felt pretty embarrassed by my failure to kill Jake.

"He had hold of my gun barrel," I pointed out. "I had no chance to aim."

"That's all right, you'll know better next time," Uncle Seth said.

Sheriff Baldy was sitting up, but he looked dazed and his face had no color.

"I picked a bad time to faint, I guess," he said.

"You've lost some blood," Uncle Seth said, politely. "You boys help me hoist Jake up on this horse—we need to take him home to the hangman."

Jake's eyes were wide open. He was staring at the sky; but he was breathing. Loading him onto the horse was like loading a big sack of oats. Once we had him tied on we helped Lester Miller climb up behind him.

I thought Sheriff Baldy was going to faint again, but he made a great effort and managed to claw his way up into the saddle.

Uncle Seth seemed to be in a high good humor— of course, it was a fine sunny day.

"Now there's a lesson in this, Jake," he said.

Jake Miller did not reply, but Uncle Seth didn't let that fact discourage him.

"The lesson is simple," Uncle Seth went on. "If you're planning an ambush you need to clear the bears out of the way first. A horse will shy at a bear nearly every time, especially if they come upon them sudden."

"I will sit astride you, as soon as I'm able, and cut your damn old Yankee throat," Jake Miller said.

"I'm feared he'll get loose—he said he'd cut our throats too," G.T. whispered.

I was a little worried on that score myself. Jake Miller seemed like the kind of man who might find a way to get loose, but as it turned out, we didn't need to worry. The circuit judge happened to be in Boone's Lick and he got Jake Miller right on the docket. A week later Jake was hung—some thought his brothers would mount a rescue mission, but they didn't. Ma wouldn't allow any of us to go to Boone's Lick on hanging day—not me, not G.T., not Neva.

"Bad elements are apt to show up on hanging day," she said.

We spent the time making lye soap. I think Cut-Nose Jones is still in jail.

**11** UNCLE Seth had coached us carefully about what to say to Ma about the gunfight, and also what *not* to say, but the coaching didn't work. Ma was not about to let one of her boys have a secret—I don't think she even allowed Uncle Seth very many secrets. She soon wormed the whole story out of G.T.—she knew the wild bandit Jake Miller had actually had his hand on my rifle barrel, a moment I'll never forget, Jake with his wild, mean eyes looking at me.

"The fact is you almost got killed, and your brother too," Ma said. "And by a handcuffed man with a broken leg."

"Almost," I said. We were at what Ma called her "laundry," a little creek that spurted into the Missouri about a hundred yards from our cabin. We also got our water from the little creek. Ma had been after Pa and Uncle Seth to dig a well, sometime when Pa was home, but he rarely *was* home, and showed no interest in well digging when he did show up.

G.T. always skipped out on laundry days. He and Uncle Seth had taken our best wagon into Boone's Lick to the blacksmith, in order to have a few things fixed before our big trip.

"I made this lye soap too strong," Ma said. "It's itching me."

Something was itching me too: the need to talk about the Stumptown raid. We had been given firm instructions not to get killed and then had almost got killed.

"I stood too close to Jake," I said. "If I'd stood farther away he could never have grabbed my gun."

Ma was standing in the creek, the brown water washing around her legs.

"Life's full of 'almost's,' Shay," she said. "Lots of things 'almost' happen—some good, some bad. You almost got killed, but you didn't. Don't be studying it too close. It's over—they hung the man. Just be smarter next time."

I wasn't so sure I *would* be smarter next time. Mostly my life happened slow, but what had occurred on the ridge above Stumptown that day hadn't happened slow. I was just now remembering certain things about it, though the fight had occurred nearly two weeks back. The night before last I remembered that Jake Miller wore a gold ring on one finger of the hand he grabbed my gun with—the fact that he wore a ring just popped into my mind as I lay on my pallet, trying to get to sleep. Maybe Jake had taken the gold ring off some of the travelers he had robbed; or maybe it was his wedding band. I saw the ring when he had his hand on my rifle barrel, but it didn't register on me for two weeks, which was a peculiar thing.

"I've had plenty of 'almost's' in *my* life," Ma said. "So has my sister Patty and so has Rosie McGee."

"Tell me about them," I said. I didn't know much about Ma's family, just that they came from Kentucky.

Ma stopped rubbing soap into one of Uncle Seth's old shirts and looked at me, with her head tilted to one side a little.

"I oughtn't to be yarning with you," she said.

"Why not?"

"Because you couldn't keep a secret if you tried," she said. "Neva or Seth or Bill Hickok could worm all you know out of you in nothing flat."

That was true, I guess. I usually just come out with whatever I knew, hoping somebody would tell me some interesting secrets in return.

I guess Ma decided she didn't much care if I told her secrets, because she smiled a little and told me a whopper of a secret.

"One 'almost' was that I almost married your uncle Seth and not your pa," she said. "And while that was happening, your pa was courting your aunt Patty, who turned him down and married your uncle Joe, who got killed in a train wreck when you were just a baby."

Ma looked at me solemnly for a moment, to see what I made of all that—then she laughed her good deep laugh and went back to soaping the shirt.

I was flabbergasted, of course. What Ma told me

that morning gave me enough to think about for the next several years. Just hearing it was not the same as understanding it, either—but Ma wasn't through. I guess she decided I was old enough to know all the family history that I had been too young to handle, before.

"My mother was married twice," Ma said. "Her first husband was a drunk who fell off a barn and broke his neck. His name was McGee, and they had one child, a girl named Rosie."

At first what Ma said didn't mean anything. I knew it was possible for a woman to marry twice, if one husband died or got killed in the war. Sometimes when Pa was up in the Indian country I wondered what Ma would do for a husband if he got killed. I even had the secret hope that if Pa *did* get killed Ma would marry Uncle Seth. Since Uncle Seth already lived with us he would know how to take care of us in case something happened to Pa.

The point about the baby girl that Granma had had with Mr. McGee, the drunk, didn't register at first. But Ma was still looking at me funny, as if she were waiting for me to solve a riddle or a puzzle or something.

"McGee. Rosie. Does that ring any bells?" she asked, with mischief in her look. Then the truth came to me like a clap of thunder: Ma was talking about the Rosie McGee who lived over the saloon and smoked cheroots at night. Ma was trying to tell me that Rosie was kin to us.

"That's right, Rosie's my half sister—she's your aunt," Ma said.

I don't remember much more about laundry

day—my thoughts were in too much confusion. I helped Ma drape the clothes on the clothesline, not even noticing when they flapped against me and got me wet. Uncle Seth had almost married Ma. Pa had tried to marry my aunt Patty; and Rosie McGee was my aunt. The more I turned these matters over and over in my mind, the more I realized that the main puzzle had to do with Ma and Pa and Uncle Seth. If Aunt Patty, the older sister, had turned Pa down, why did Ma pick him? After all, she already had Uncle Seth, who was probably just as partial to her then as he was now.

Ma could see that I was wrestling with a lot of complicated thoughts: it just seemed to amuse her. I tried to work up a set of questions I could ask her, but Ma put me off with a look. I had the feeling that she had said what she wanted to say about these matters and had no intention of saying another word—or at least not a word that made sense to a person my age, who didn't know much.

Next day when she and Neva and I were in the garden, digging spuds and putting them in a sack, several crows came flapping over the barn—they soon flew on toward the river, cawing as they went.

Ma pitched a potato into the sack and gave me a little smile.

"I pity the fate of the carrion crow," she said. "Those black birds mate for life."

"Who cares what a crow does?" Neva said. A little later she took herself off to Boone's Lick. The news was that Wild Bill Hickok was back in town.

**12** W O M E N will even sniff bread," Uncle Seth informed me. We were out hunting Little Nicky, the biting mule. He had had a wild, biting fit during the night; in order to get clear of him Old Sam and the other mules had kicked down the pen and went running loose. We had got back six of them, but Little Nicky and a mule named Henry Clay were still missing. They had gone in the general direction of Stumptown, which led Uncle Seth to speculate that Little Nicky might have gone back to try and bite the bear.

"Why do women sniff bread?" I asked. It was something I often noticed Mu doing, when she made bread.

"To see if it's fresh, I expect," Uncle Seth said.

"I have never sniffed bread in my life, which is the difference between me and a woman.

"And when a woman comes to decide who to marry it comes down to the same test," he added.

"You mean they sniff men?" I asked. I could not imagine what it would feel like to have a woman sniff me.

"Yes, to determine if the fellow's fresh," Uncle Seth said. "I guess I don't smell fresh, which is why I'm a bachelor still."

"That's pretty peculiar," I said.

"Oh no, I expect it's a fine method," Uncle Seth said, trying to make out Little Nicky's tracks on the trail.

"Women don't know why they choose who they choose," he went on. "If they say otherwise it's a lie. A good fresh scent's probably the best thing they got to go on."

I was wanting to tell him—since we were on the subject—that I knew he had once courted Ma, but seeing how partial he was to her still, I wasn't sure how he'd take it.

"Damn a mule that will wander," he said. "I could be in Boone's Lick, playing cards and winning money, if I wasn't halfway to Stumptown, looking for a goddamn ungrateful biting mule."

We had just heard the news that Sheriff Baldy Stone had quit his job. That bullet that bounced off his saddle and hit him in the stomach had done more damage than it seemed at the time. Sheriff Baldy had so much trouble just holding down his food that he lacked the energy to go out and arrest bandits. I thought it was a pity. I liked Sheriff Baldy, although his untimely faint had nearly got me killed.

G.T. was on the mule hunt too, only he was lagging so far behind he couldn't take part in the conversation.

"Maybe they'll make Mr. Hickok sheriff," I said.

"Oh no, Bill couldn't be bothered to keep a jail," Uncle Seth said. "Anyway, he's a half criminal himself, which is what you find in a good many of these sheriffs.

"I expect they'd offer the job to me, if I wasn't leaving," he went on. "It's bad luck for the town that Mary Margaret's got her mind set on this expedition. She's determined to find Dick if it kills us—which it might."

"I expect Pa will be glad to see us," I said. I didn't want to think about us all getting killed—in my thinking it would just be a nice fall trip, with lots of buffalo for us to chase.

Uncle Seth gave me a strange look, when I suggested that Pa would be glad to see us.

"Shay, you have not been around your father enough to figure out the first thing about him," Uncle Seth said. "The truth is he *won't* be glad to see us—it's more likely to make him boiling mad."

"Why?" I asked. "We're his family."

"*That's* why!" Uncle Seth said. "One reason Dick's a wagoner is because he's got no tolerance for family life. Your pa ain't sociable—at least not with white people. He didn't leave me behind because I'm a little gimpy—that was just his excuse.

He never wanted me hauling with him anyway. Too much company."

"If he don't like white people, who does he like?" I asked.

"Cheyenne Indians, maybe a few Sioux," Uncle Seth said. "I have no doubt he's got a plump little squaw to cook him dog stew and keep him warm when it's chilly."

It seemed I was learning something new about my family almost every day now. I always thought we were just an ordinary family—and maybe we were; but then, maybe we weren't.

"If Pa doesn't want us to come, then why are we going?" I asked.

Uncle Seth never answered that question. We weren't far from where we'd seen the bear, a fact which made G.T. nervous. He came thundering up to join us about that time, but what really distracted Uncle Seth was something he noticed on the ground.

"Somebody's found our mules," he said. He dismounted and walked around on the trail for a few minutes, studying the tracks. There were a lot of tracks, but they were just a blur to me and even more of a blur to G.T.

"Well, Little Nicky ain't traveling alone anymore, and neither is Henry Clay," Uncle Seth said, after a thorough examination of the trail. "That damn Newt Tebbit must have come upon them and decided he'd help himself to two fine mules—the damn scoundrel.

"I should have whacked him harder, when I

whacked him," he went on, swinging back on his horse.

"What makes you think it's him—it could be anybody," G.T. said.

"I was not born a fool, like you, G.T.," Uncle Seth said. "I noticed when we were following the Tebbits that Newt's horse was shod. Few people around here can afford to keep their horses shod, though it was common until the war. Bill Hickok keeps his shod, but then he's in a profession that might require rapid flight and a surefooted horse. But Bill ain't a mule thief. Newt Tebbit's our mule thief."

"I guess we'll have to get up another posse," G.T. said.

"Having to educate you is a heavy burden, G.T.," Uncle Seth said. "We *are* the posse, this time. Be sure there's a cartridge in your gun."

Then he went loping off. Soon we were past Stumptown and were in the wooded country where the Millers were said to live. Uncle Seth didn't study the tracks much—he just kept going.

"I wish I'd brought a biscuit," G.T. said.

We were well into the wooded country before Uncle Seth slowed down.

"I believe some of the Tebbits are married to some of the Millers, and vice versa," Uncle Seth said. "I expect we'll find the bunch of them in camp together. I feel confident we can lick a barnful of Tebbits, but I'm a little worried about Ronnie Miller, who's said to be a good shot. He's the one whose horse flipped, remember?"

I remembered the horse flipping, of course, but I had never had a good look at the rider—I just remembered that he hadn't moved for a while.

"I'll deal with Ronnie, if he shows fight," Uncle Seth said.

About that time we heard Little Nicky neigh.

"He smells our mules," Uncle Seth said. "If he runs up and tries to bite one of you, get a halter on him."

"I smell something cooking," G.T. said. "Maybe they've killed a beef."

"Or a mule," Uncle Seth said.

I knew that some of the families that camped or homesteaded around in the woods lived poorly—the more so since the war, when nobody in the vicinity of Boone's Lick suffered from too much to eat—but I forgot all about being part of a posse when we rode into the Millers' camp and saw all the skin-and-bones people. There were so many children that it might have been a schoolhouse—only there was no proper house, just three or four shacks with no windows or doors. Uncle Seth later said that he counted sixteen children, none of them older than ten and many of them babies, in the crawling or toddling state. Uncle Seth had guessed right when he said it was a mule cooking: Henry Clay, fully skinned out, was hanging from the skinning pole. Parts of him were already in the stew pots and a haunch was spitted over a big campfire. Several women were tending to the pots and campfires, while Newt Tebbit and Ronnie Miller cut up the meat. At our house Ma fought constantly to

keep us fairly clean, marching us off to the creek
for baths at least once a week, and sweeping and
doing laundry to combat dirt; but the men and
women at the Miller camp had long since given up
trying to be clean. Most of them were black with
filth. Several hounds came out and yapped at us—
they were as skinny as the people. It was plain that
the Millers and the Tebbits lived off the wild: deer-
skins and pigs' heads were scattered here and
there.

Newt and Percy Tebbit were both there, cutting
Henry Clay into strips of jerky. Lester Miller was
there—he had been let off light by the circuit
judge, and also Lyle and Jody, the two men who
had hobbled away after the bear got them pitched
off their horses.

Several rifles were in sight, leaned up against
stumps here and there, but no one made a move for
them, when we rode in. Little Nicky was tied to a
bush not far away.

Ronnie Miller, who seemed to be the boss of the
family, was sitting on a stump, sharpening his
knife on a whetstone. He didn't seem particularly
hostile, nor did anyone else. Probably they were all
so starved down that all they could think about was
eating our mule, Henry Clay.

"It's surprising how quick a knife will go dull
when you're cutting up a tough mule," Ronnie
said.

"Yes, or any large critter," Uncle Seth said, in a
friendly tone. "I believe buffalo are the worst—an
old buffalo is a damn task to cut up."

"That's a pleasure I've not had, Seth," Ronnie Miller said. "You're a little too late to rescue your big mule. As you can see we've got hungry mouths to feed. Besides, you're the man who cost us three horses, including one that nearly broke my neck, it threw me so far. On the other hand, you did us a big favor when you caught Jake—he was a terror to live with—anybody here can tell you that.

"I would have hung the son of a bitch myself, if I could have ever caught him off guard," he added.

"It's no surprise that Jake wasn't well liked in the family," Uncle Seth said. "He cursed all of you thoroughly while they were settling the hang rope around his neck."

Just then there was a screech from Percy Tebbit, who had sidled up beside Little Nicky. I imagine he meant to leap on Nicky and run off with him, before we could stop him, but Little Nicky, who had been baring his teeth at Percy, reached down and bit him right in the hand.

"Dern, he's nearly bitten my hand off!" Percy said, blood spurting from his hand.

"It's unwise to approach this particular mule unless you have a stout club," Uncle Seth said. "He'll bite anybody that comes in reach."

He rode over and untied Nicky, an action that drew unfriendly looks from some of the Millers and the Tebbits.

"You see, I told you we should have shot both mules," Newt Tebbit said.

"We *had* intended to eat both those animals, since we found them running free," Ronnie Miller said—still, he didn't strike a very fierce pose. I don't think he expected Uncle Seth to just give him two mules free, and if he had tried to start a fight there were several women and children right in the way.

"Newt's right—if you wanted to eat him you should have shot him," Uncle Seth said. "Though I despise a biting mule I have to take this one home. I can give you a fine tip about that bear, though— he's got himself a den under that little rocky spur, about two miles west of Stumptown. If I was you I'd smoke him out. A bear is just as tasty as a mule."

"They can't bite much worse than this son of a bitch bites, neither," Percy Tebbit said, trying to wring the blood off his hand.

"Did you really see that bear go into a den?" G.T. asked, once we had left with Nicky.

"Mind your own business, G.T.," Uncle Seth said, and that was all the answer he ever made.

Ma was not happy about the loss of Henry Clay, either.

"How do you know *we* won't need to eat a mule, before we're through?" Ma asked.

If Uncle Seth made any answer I didn't hear it.

**13** P E O P L E think Bill Hickok can't miss, but he *can* miss," Uncle Seth said. We were walking to Boone's Lick. Ma had sent me off to the dry goods store to get a thimble—she was always losing thimbles. Her theory was that baby Marcy was swallowing them, though we could never catch her at it. When he saw me leaving, Uncle Seth fell in with me, although he had no particular errand—none that he mentioned to me, anyway.

"People think Bill always gets his man, but he don't," he went on—the thought of Mr. Hickok's big reputation seemed to irritate him for some reason.

"Look at what happened when he took off after Little Billy Perkins," Uncle Seth reminded me. "It was clear in a minute that Little Billy had the faster mount, but would Bill quit? Not him! Little Billy swam the Missouri River twice and then headed west—he outran Bill all the way to the Smoky Hill River, which is in Kansas—and Bill still didn't get him. They say Bill Hickok wore out three horses before he admitted defeat."

I think Uncle Seth meant to leave me at the dry goods store, to purchase my thimble, while he went on to the saloon, which was only three doors away, but just as I was about to peel off from him, who should step out of the store but Rosie McGee. She was surely pretty—now that I knew we were kin I could see that she resembled Ma, in some ways. They had the same black hair, and the same gray eyes and long fingers. Of course, Rosie looked more like a town lady than Ma did. There was a time before the war when Ma had gone into town now and then, to socials and quilting bees and that kind of thing; but the war dragged on and life at the freight yard got so hard that Ma rarely indulged in visits to Boone's Lick anymore.

"Hello, Seth—I hear you're leaving me," Rosie said, with a little smile. She was carrying a fan, although it wasn't hot. The fan looked as if it was made of pearls, or something.

"It's likely—there's talk of a trip to try and locate Dick," Uncle Seth admitted.

"You could introduce me to your nephew, the wagoner's lad," Rosie said. "I hope he's quick on his feet, if you're heading into the Cheyenne country."

"Well, his name is Sherman but we all call him Shay," Uncle Seth said.

"You can call him what you like but *I* intend to call him Sherman," Rosie said. "I don't like these little names."

She offered me her hand and I took it—I didn't know if I was supposed to bow, or what.

"Pleased to meet you—I guess I'm your nephew, besides," I said—it startled Uncle Seth so badly he nearly fell off the steps.

If Rosie was surprised by my remark she didn't show it.

"Why, so you are," she said. "You're my nephew, but how did you know?"

"Ma told me," I informed her. "She said you were her half sister, so that makes me a half nephew, I guess."

"No halves about it, Sherman," Rosie said immediately. "You're my nephew and I'm your aunt. This is better than beating Bill Hickok at cards. Or any of these bumblers around here."

She smiled at me—such a big, open smile—and I felt something lift inside me. Up to then, there had been no one for me but Ma—everything that came from women came from her; but that had just changed. I didn't know how much I'd get to see of my aunt Rosie, but I hoped it would be a lot. Right off I started liking her so much that I began to wish we weren't going on our trip. Of course, I wanted to see Pa, and the wonderful country up-river, but I was hoping we wouldn't have to start too soon, just when I had my new aunt to visit. At least, I hoped I would get to visit her—and I had hardly made the wish before it came true.

"Seth, you run along now—I see you've got whiskey and dominoes on your mind," Aunt Rosie said. "I'm going to take my new nephew Sherman home with me—we've got a lot of lost time to make up."

For some reason Uncle Seth looked discombobulated. The vein popped out on top of his nose and his whole face turned red. The news about Aunt Rosie and I being related seemed to have upset him in some way. Of course, it was no trick for Ma to upset him. She was always doing it. Evidently Aunt Rosie had the same power.

"This boy's been sent on an errand—he'd best not be neglecting his errands," Uncle Seth said.

"Oh, what errand?" Rosie asked.

"Just buying a thimble—Ma lost hers," I said.

"Shucks, I've got twenty thimbles right upstairs here," Aunt Rosie said. "I'll just give your ma one and save her three cents."

"Okay," I said.

"Now, this is a mighty hasty arrangement," Uncle Seth began.

"So what?" Rosie said, cutting him short. "I finally met my nephew and I want to visit with him. What's wrong with that?"

Uncle Seth didn't answer. It was plain that he didn't approve of my going off with Rosie, but he couldn't think of a quick reason why I shouldn't.

"Just remember you've got that harness to polish—now don't neglect it!" he said, before stomping off to the saloon

I didn't know what to make of Uncle Seth's behavior.

"We never polish the harness," I told Rosie. "I don't even know what I'm supposed to polish it with."

Aunt Rosie just laughed. "Seth's so mad he could spit," she said, and then she hooked her arm in mine and led me down the street and up the steps to her room over the saloon. We were only a few yards behind Uncle Seth, but he never looked back.

"Mad—he's blazing!" Aunt Rosie said, and laughed a deep hearty laugh, like Ma's. If I had nothing else to go on I would have picked them as sisters just from the sound of their laughter.

Aunt Rosie led me upstairs to her room, which was nicer than any other room I had ever been in. There was a settee and a chair, and a little table with a mirror on it, and a fine bed with a pretty coverlet—the coverlet might have been satin, I'm not sure. The windows had curtains—if you looked out one you could see the Missouri River meandering away to the west.

"My, my, you're certainly a handsome youth," Aunt Rosie said, letting me look around to my heart's content. She went to the table, opened up a little sewing box, and handed me two thimbles to take to Ma.

"One to fulfill your commission, and one to spare," she said.

I took the thimbles and put them in my pocket. I was thrilled to be talking to Aunt Rosie but I couldn't quite get Uncle Seth out of my mind.

"I don't know what I done to make Uncle Seth get so upset," I said.

"Oh, he's just jealous," Rosie said. "He wanted me to entertain *him* and here I am entertaining *you*. So he's having a little fit, as gentlemen will."

That puzzled me—I didn't know what to say.

"Seth Cecil will sulk and pout, if he isn't made over constantly," Aunt Rosie said. "Your pa's even worse in that regard. Do folks tell you you look like your pa?"

"I don't know many people who even *know* Pa," I admitted. "He's gone so much I can't remember what he looks like myself."

"Yes, Dick's a rover—I told your ma that, before she married him," Aunt Rosie said. "You look just like him, only not so devilish—do you like whiskey?"

"I don't know—I've not been allowed any," I said. "Once Uncle Seth brought home some Rebel beer, but it didn't have much taste."

"I'll pass on Rebel beer," Aunt Rosie said. "My weakness is whiskey."

There was a bottle and a few glasses on the little table by the mirror. Aunt Rosie poured a glass about half full, for me, and one a little bit fuller for herself.

"I try to limit myself to a glass a day, but sometimes I slip a little," she said, handing me a glass. "Don't gulp it down now—just take a sip."

But I was nervous—despite Aunt Rosie's warning I took a full gulp of the whiskey. It felt like scalding lye had just gone down my throat. The heat of it brought tears to my eyes—Aunt Rosie had to pound me on the back so I wouldn't choke.

"That wasn't exactly a sip," she said. "But it was a start."

A little later I felt a heat in my stomach, as if someone had shoveled a few coals inside me. I sipped a little more whiskey, and a little more still, and soon ceased to feel my legs. It was as if my body ended at my belly. Aunt Rosie sat on one end of the settee, and I sat on the other. She drank and I drank but our glasses never seemed to quite get empty. Somehow Aunt Rosie managed to refill them without my noticing. At one point I noticed that the bottle was empty, but when I looked again it was full.

"It ain't often I get this full of family feeling," Aunt Rosie said. "I want you to throw a bottle for me. Seth don't like to admit it but I can shoot as well as he can. Come on—I'll show you."

By then it was nearly sundown. Aunt Rosie took a rifle out of the closet behind her bed. She gave me an empty whiskey bottle and we went out on the little landing behind her room. I threw the bottle as high as I could. Aunt Rosie shot, there was a crack, and little pieces of glass rained into a kind of weedy lot behind the saloon. I looked down and saw Wild Bill Hickok standing below, watching us.

"How's that, Mr. Sureshot?" Aunt Rosie cried out. Mr. Hickok made no comment, or none that I can remember.

Aunt Rosie helped me down the stairs, giggling

at how clumsy I had become. On the way home my feet kept wanting to get tangled up with one another. I tried to walk normally but my left foot kept trying to cross over to where my right foot ought to be. My left foot was the bad foot—I got so annoyed with it that I wanted to shoot it off. At one point I found myself thirty yards off the trail, in some bushes, though I knew the way home perfectly well.

When I finally got to our cabin I tried to walk through the door but missed and bumped my head on the doorsill. Ma and Neva were at the kitchen table, peeling spuds. I had to make three runs at it before I finally got through the door. Ma and Neva just sat there looking at me, as if I were someone they didn't know.

"What's wrong with him—the oaf!" Neva said.

"Oh, nothing—he's probably just been drinking whiskey with his Aunt Rosie," Ma said.

Then she stood up and ruffled my hair a little, like she had done when I was younger. For some reason I felt like crying, but Ma seemed to think it was all funny. She laughed, but Neva didn't.

I was up vomiting most of the night.

There was no sign of Uncle Seth.

**14** T H R E E days after I got drunk that first time Uncle Seth showed up at the cabin again. He walked in with a lordly air—it was his usual air—but he looked as if he'd spent his time in a pigsty. His clothes were filthy and one of his ears was red.

If Ma was put out by his absence she didn't show it, which didn't mean she was prepared to accept his appearance. G.T. had managed to get in a fight somewhere, that afternoon. He looked as bunged up as Uncle Seth. The sight of them set Granpa Crackenthorpe cackling.

"Here's two fellows who got themselves whipped," he said.

"You shut up or I'll stab you in the leg again," G.T. said.

Granpa started looking for his cap-and-ball pistol, but before he found it Ma gave the two of them some soap and told them to go to the creek and get clean. By the time they came back, considerably cleaner, Granpa had found his pistol, but Ma took it away from him and didn't give it back until he had cooled down considerably.

"I may have to put you on the street yet," she informed Granpa—it was a threat that took the fight out of Granpa real quick.

"She'd let an old man starve," he said, to the cabin at large, but no one paid him the slightest mind.

For the last three days Ma had been stuffing things in sacks and boxes—potatoes, onions, clothes, pots, tools—anything that she thought might be useful on a trip across the prairies. No sooner would one of us get through with one chore than she would drag up another sack and tell us to put it in the wagon.

At first I didn't really believe we were going to look for Pa. It just seemed like one of the notions Ma sometimes got in her head. Once she had a notion that we ought to raise turkeys, but the coyotes and foxes and bobcats soon got all the turkeys.

Besides, why would we need to drag a wagon off across the plains to look for Pa, when he always showed up in Boone's Lick of his own accord once every year or two? He'd come and stay two or three days and then go. Usually, a month or so after one of Pa's visits, Ma's belly would begin to swell, and eventually there'd be another baby.

That had always seemed to be Pa and Ma's way—of course, when Pa wasn't around, Uncle

Seth looked after us pretty well. Why go bother Pa if he didn't want to be bothered?

G.T. and I thought Uncle Seth would finally talk her out of the move, but Neva didn't agree.

"You oafs, we're going next week," Neva claimed. She had been calling us oafs for the past few weeks—once Neva found a word she liked she tended to work it hard, until she found a new word she liked better.

It was beginning to look as if Neva was right. Our wagon was nearly full of sacks and boxes, and it still had to hold all of us, including Granpa. The cabin looked so bare, from all the stuff we'd moved out, that the sight of it seemed to help Uncle Seth recover his sense of humor.

"We're down to the dirt floors, here," he said to Ma. "There's plenty of places outdoors that look more comfortable than this."

"We won't have to be uncomfortable long," Ma informed him. "Come Monday morning early I'd like to be on the move."

"Good Lord, that's just two days, Mary Margaret," Uncle Seth said. "I'll be hard pressed to get my affairs settled up in just two days."

Ma didn't seem concerned.

"What you can't settle you'll just have to leave," she told him.

"Mary Margaret, we've lived here for sixteen years," he reminded her. "That's a long time."

"It is, but it'll be over in two days," Ma said. "And the only people I'll miss are those in the graveyard: my mother and my sister and my boys."

When Ma mentioned the graveyard even Uncle Seth knew it was no time for jokes.

"I trust you've found us a boat," Ma said. "I would like to make some of this trip by boat—I fear it would be too much wear and tear on the wagons to do it all overland."

"Not to mention the wear and tear on the mules and the people," Uncle Seth said.

Just then, through the door, we heard the click of buggy wheels, coming up the trail. Ma's first thought was of Uncle Seth.

"Are you in trouble, Seth?" she asked. "Did you kill somebody in your brawl?"

Neva, who was curious about everything, had already run out the door.

"It's Aunt Rosie!" she yelled.

Ma was closest to the door. "She's hurt—go see to her, Seth," Ma said.

There was such alarm in her voice that we all ran outside. Aunt Rosie was stretched across the seat of the buggy in a bloody dress. She was so beat up I hardly recognized her—both eyes were swollen shut. The blood was from a split lip. The old buggy man who met the trains and riverboats was driving. When Uncle Seth tried to ease Aunt Rosie out of the buggy she gave a sharp cry.

"Ribs," she said.

"Shay, go to the creek and get a bucket of water," Ma said.

"I'll kill whoever done this," Uncle Seth said.

"No you won't—the sheriff done it," Rosie said. "Joe Tate. He's not like Sheriff Baldy."

"Hurry, Shay—mind me," Ma said. "We need the water."

By the time I got back with the bucket of water Ma had made Aunt Rosie a comfortable pallet by the fireplace. She soon had water heated and it wasn't long before she had cleaned the blood off her sister.

"I can't do much about the ribs," Ma said.

"I'll go fetch the doctor, then," Uncle Seth said.

He was standing over Rosie with a dark look on his face.

"Don't let him go, Mary," Rosie said at once. "Send Sherman."

"I suppose I'm free to go to town if I want to," Uncle Seth said, but both women shook their heads. Even Neva shook her head, though I don't know what Neva thought *she* knew about it.

"No you ain't—not when you're this mad," Ma said.

They stared at one another, over Aunt Rosie: Ma and Uncle Seth. I could see he was strongly inclined to go out the door. I didn't know why a sheriff would want to beat up Aunt Rosie, but I agreed with Uncle Seth that he deserved to be killed for it.

"Seth, you just calm down," Rosie said—her voice wasn't very strong. It reminded me of Sheriff Baldy's voice, just before he fainted.

"Calm down, with you half dead?" Uncle Seth said. "I guess I won't—not until Joe Tate's answered for this deed."

"That new preacher stirred him up—it's happened before," Aunt Rosie said. "New preachers always think they have to start preaching against whores."

"I suppose it helps them at the collection plate," Ma said.

"Preachers . . . they should shut their damn traps!" Uncle Seth said. "But a preacher couldn't stir up a sheriff to do such as this unless the sheriff was mean to begin with. Joe Tate's just a damn bully."

"Listen to me, Seth," Ma said. "We're leaving this place in two days. It may be that we'll never be back. We have a long trip to make and we'll need your help. I can't allow you to march off and shoot the sheriff, or pistol-whip him, or whatever you have in mind."

"Plenty, that's what I have in mind," Uncle Seth said. He cast his eyes down, so as not to have to face Ma, and started for the door.

"Seth!" Ma said—Ma could speak stern when she needed to, but I had never heard her speak quite *this* stern.

Uncle Seth stopped, but he didn't turn around.

"If you walk out that door I'm through with you," Ma said. "I wash my hands of you. I swear I'll take these younguns and go find Dick myself, and if we all get scalped, so be it."

Uncle Seth stood where he was for a minute, stiff and annoyed.

"Mary, are you teasing?" he asked, finally.

"What do you think, Rosie?" Ma asked. "Am I teasing?"

"She's not teasing, Seth," Rosie said.

Then she laughed a funny little laugh that must have caused her ribs to twinge, because she coughed in pain at the end of the laugh.

"Mary Margaret's not much of a teaser," she said.

"Oh, she can tease with the best of them, when the mood's on her," Uncle Seth said.

"Leave Joe Tate alone!" Ma said. "We don't need worse trouble than we've got."

"I've never been much of a hand for taking orders from females," Uncle Seth said.

There was a silence that wasn't comfortable—such a tense silence that even Neva shut up, for once.

Then Uncle Seth turned from the door as if he had never intended to go out it. He made as if he felt light as a feather, all of a sudden—though none of us believed that. Still, we were all glad when the silence ended.

"There's Rosie McGee," he said, in a softer tone. "What do we do with her, when we start this big trip you're determined to go on?"

"Why, take her with us, of course," Ma said. "Did you suppose I planned to leave my sister in a place like this?"

That surprised us all—and pleased me, I must say. I wouldn't be having to leave Aunt Rosie so quickly.

That seemed to ease Uncle Seth's mind.

"All right, Mary Margaret," he said. "But Joe Tate don't know how lucky he is."

"Go on—get the doctor, Shay," Ma said, and I went.

I ran all the way down the hill but then had to look in three saloons before I found Doc, who was a little tipsy. When I mentioned that it was Rosie who was hurt he got right up and came with me, but he had such trouble hitching his nag to the buggy that I finally did it for him.

"Let's hurry, Rosie's a prize," he said, offering me the reins. Twice more, on the way, he mentioned that Aunt Rosie was a prize. He doctored her cuts pretty well but shook his head over the matter of the ribs.

"They'll just have to mend in their own time, Rosie," he said.

The next night, while making his midnight rounds, Sheriff Joe Tate got trampled by a runaway horse. The horse came bearing down on him in a dark alley and knocked him winding—one hip was broken, plus his collarbone and several ribs; besides that, he was unconscious for several hours and could make no report on the horse or the rider, if there had been a rider.

I don't know what Ma or Aunt Rosie thought about the matter, but G.T. and I suspected Uncle Seth, who had gone to the saloon as usual, that night. When G.T. asked him about it, Uncle Seth just looked bored.

"He should have carried a lantern," Uncle Seth said. "Any fool who wanders the streets at midnight without a lantern ought to expect to get trampled by a horse, I don't care if he is a lawman. It's only common sense to carry a light."

He never changed his story, either. To this day I don't know if Uncle Seth was on the horse that trampled Sheriff Joe Tate.

**15** T H E morning before we left I went down to the lots alone about sunrise, to feed the mules—I always liked being out early, if I was awake. The world just seemed so fresh, in the first hour of the day. The river, usually, would be white with mist—then the big red sun would swell up over the world's edge and the light would touch the church spire and the few roofs of Boone's Lick. All the roosters in town would be crowing, and our three roosters too. The mules seemed glad to see me, though I imagine they would have been glad to see anyone who fed them. In the wintertime the frost would sparkle on the ground and on the trees. Sometimes, when I got back to the cabin, Ma would allow me a cup of coffee, once she was satisfied that I had finished my chores.

G.T. was a late sleeper, and Neva too. Sometimes I'd get to sit alone with Ma for a minute, before the day got started.

Unless the weather was wet Uncle Seth slept outside, in a little camp he had made not far from the cabin. He had spent so much time on the open prairies, with the stars to look at, that he could no longer tolerate the confinements of a roof.

"I'd like to spend as many nights as possible looking straight up at heaven," he said.

"Looking is all you'll get to do," Ma said. "You're too bad a sinner to expect to get any closer."

I didn't understand that, since about the most sinful thing Uncle Seth did was get drunk—since he was sleeping outdoors anyway, his getting drunk didn't bother anybody. Ma wasn't churchly, anyway—maybe her calling him a sinner was just a joke between them.

This morning, though, I got a kind of lonely feeling as I was walking down to the lots. The lonely feeling stayed with me all through my chores, although it was a lovely morning. I saw several skeins of Canada geese flying north, above the river, in the direction we would soon be going ourselves, the whole bunch of us, from baby Marcy to Granpa Crackenthorpe, piled in our wagon, on top of the sacks. Uncle Seth had arranged for a flatboat to take us all the way to Omaha, which was way upriver, I guess.

"After that, it'll be chancy travel," Uncle Seth informed us all. "I may not be able to find a boat willing to haul four mules and a bunch of crazy people into the Sioux country."

The geese soon circled around and landed on the river—it was the wrong time of year for them to be going very far north. But thinking about the north just fit in with my lonely feeling. I had never lived anyplace but our cabin. I knew every tree and bush for a mile or two around, knew the way to Boone's Lick, knew most of the folks who worked in the stores. I knew the river, too—in the summer I could even figure out where the big catfish fed.

Now we were leaving the only place G.T. and Neva and I had ever lived. The fact of it almost made me queasy, for a while, though part of me was excited at the thought of traveling up the river and over the plains, into the country where the wild Indians lived, where there were elk and grizzly bears and lots of buffalo. It would be a big adventure—maybe Ma would find Pa and satisfy her feelings about his behavior—that was a part of it I just didn't understand, since there was no sign that Pa was behaving any differently than he had ever done.

Still, I was leaving my *home*—the big adventure was still just thoughts in my head, but our home was our place. The river, the town, the mules, the stables, the cabin, Uncle Seth's little camp under the stars, the wolf's den G.T. and I found, the geese overhead, the ducks that paddled around in big clusters along the shallows of the river, even the crawdads that G.T. trapped or the turtles that sank down, missing their heads, after Uncle Seth shot them—the white frost in the fall and the sun swelling up from beyond the edge of the world: all that, we were leaving, and a sadness got mixed in with the thought of the big adventure we would have. All around Boone's Lick there were cabins that people had just left and never came back to— many had emptied out because of the war. Once the people left, the woods and the weeds, the snakes and the spiders just seemed to take the cabins back. Pretty soon a few logs would roll down, and the roof would cave in. Within a year or two even a sturdy cabin would begin to look like a place nobody was ever going to come back to, or live in again.

The thought that *our* cabin might cave in, become a place of snakes and spiders, owls and rats, made me feel lonely inside, because it had been such a cheerful place. It *had* been, despite the babies dying and Granma dying and Ma's sister Polly dying. Though I was there when the dyings happened I didn't remember them clearly; what I remembered was Granpa playing the fiddle and Ma singing, and her and Uncle Seth dancing around the table, on nights when Uncle Seth was in a dancing mood, which he seemed to get in at least once a week. G.T. fancied that he could play the Jew's harp, so he would join in, wailing, when Granpa played his fiddle.

"I won't live in a downcast house," Ma said to us, more than once. "It's not fair to the young ones."

Even so I felt downcast when I looked at the

wagon full of sacks and boxes and realized we were really leaving. Our cabin would soon be just another abandoned place—if we didn't find Pa and get back to Boone's Lick soon, it would begin to fall down and cave in, like all the other abandoned cabins people had left.

I guess everyone must have felt a little bit like I was feeling, that day. There was usually a lot of talk going on in our family—joshing, bickering, fussing—but everyone kind of kept quiet that last day—kept to themselves. Ma had an absent look in her eye, as if she had already left and was just waiting for the day and the night to pass, so we could load ourselves in the wagon and head for the boat. Aunt Rosie had made good friends with baby Marcy—they were so thick already that Marcy could hardly even tolerate Uncle Seth, a fact that irked him a little. The day seemed a lot longer than most days—it passed with everybody mostly being quiet. Aunt Rosie's bruises had all turned purple, and she had to move carefully when she stood up.

"This baby thinks I'm a clown, with purple eyes," Aunt Rosie said. "I expect that's why she likes me."

"She used to like me, before you turned her head," Uncle Seth said.

There was a full moon that night. G.T. wanted to go coon hunting, but I wasn't in the mood. Ma spent most of the night in the graveyard, sitting on her bench—Aunt Rosie came out and sat with her for a while. She brought Marcy, who made quite a bit of progress with her crawling—she was soon crawling around amid the little gravestones. Uncle Seth was restless—he didn't approve of Marcy being allowed to crawl wherever she wanted to go.

"You ought to keep better watch—she could get on a snake," I heard him say—but the two women paid him no mind. Marcy kept crawling and Uncle Seth finally walked down to Boone's Lick, to visit the saloons.

**16** I T takes just a short minute to leave a place, even though you've lived there for years. Ma fed us each a bowl of mush and told us to get in the wagon. G.T. and I helped Aunt Rosie climb up—she was mighty sore. Ma handed her baby Marcy. Granpa had strapped on his pistol, in order to be prepared for attack, but once in the wagon he didn't say much. Since we were just going down to the docks to locate our boat, Neva and G.T. and I walked. Sometimes we'd visit the docks two or three times a day, just to see what was going on. Usually somebody would have caught a big fish, or a paddle steamer would have blown its boiler, or some soldiers would be standing around, waiting for a boat to take them to one of the forts upriver, or some men would be gambling with dice—something worth watching would usually be happening at the docks.

Ma shut the door to the cabin and that was that—she didn't look back.

"Scoot over," she told Uncle Seth, who had climbed up on the wagon seat. He had been waiting, holding the reins to the team. We had sold two mules to get traveling money, but we still had Nicky and Old Sam and Ben and Montgomery, which was more mule power than it really took to pull one wagon. Ma said it was better to have too many rather than not enough.

Uncle Seth had not been talking much—if he had had a long night in the saloon, his tongue didn't begin to get loose until around noon—but he was taken by surprise when Ma told him to scoot over.

"Why?" he asked.

"Because I'm driving the team," Ma said.

"Why?" Uncle Seth asked again. "What do you know about handling mules?"

"Enough," Ma said.

Aunt Rosie thought that was funny—she laughed—but it seemed to make Granpa Crackenthorpe a little anxious. He began to work his gums.

"It's a wonder he don't take a bed slat to you," he said.

Once he saw that Ma was determined to drive, Uncle Seth scooted over and handed her the reins.

"I didn't raise her up to be that sassy," Granpa assured Uncle Seth.

"I guess it must just be a natural talent, then," Uncle Seth said.

Ma gave no sign of having heard either comment. She clucked at the mules and we left our home. Ma set a brisk pace too—even Neva, a fast walker, had to trot to keep up with the wagon as we went spinning down to Boone's Lick and right on through it. Newt and Percy Tebbit were sitting in front of the jail. They both looked surprised to see us go whistling by. Percy was so surprised he dropped the plug of tobacco he had been about to stick in his mouth. Uncle Seth didn't say a word to the Tebbits and they didn't say a word to him. Sally, Uncle Seth's gray mare, who was tied to the back of the wagon, whinnied when we passed the jail, and a horse that was hitched outside the saloon whinnied back.

"That's Bill Hickok's nag—I guess he's having himself a toddy," Uncle Seth said.

"I don't see the boat," Ma said. "I see a canoe, but we can't get this wagon in a canoe. Where's our boat, Seth?"

We could all see that there was no flatboat waiting for us.

Uncle Seth was as startled as anyone to discover that our boat was missing. There were usually several boats in sight, going upstream and downstream, big boats and small, barges and steamers of various kinds. Sometimes Neva and I would sit on the dock most of the day, just watching boats. If they were going downstream they were bound for St. Louis, where Neva and I planned to go someday—that would have to be when we were grown.

This morning, though, there were no boats on

the river at all. A canoe with a few blankets in it was pulled up onshore and an Indian in an old hat, wearing leggings and a thin shirt, stood by it, untangling a fishing line.

From the docks we could see a long distance, up- and downriver, but no boats were in sight.

"This is a vexation for sure," Ma said to Uncle Seth. "You told me they'd be here."

"Well, they're late, the scamps," Uncle Seth said, with an embarrassed look. Here we were ready to travel hundreds of miles and find our pa—only there was no boat, or even anyone to ask about the boat except the one Indian man.

"Ask him if he's seen our boat, Seth," Ma said.

"Why would he be able to see something that we can't see?" Uncle Seth inquired. I thought it was a good point. There was just no boat in sight—the Indian couldn't change that.

Four mules, a gray mare, and a wagon full of people make a certain amount of noise, and the Indian naturally heard it. He turned and looked at us—his look was not unfriendly, nor was it friendly, either. He was more interested in getting his fishing line untangled than he was in us—I suppose that was normal, since he'd never met us.

"If you don't ask him I will," Ma said. "Here we are ready to go and our boat's lost."

"People who work on water don't keep time as well as people who work on land," Uncle Seth explained.

"Well, they should!" Ma said. She stared down the river, as if she could make the boat appear just by staring— only she was wrong.

"I expect they're just stuck on a sandbar, around the curve, and will be here as soon as they get unstuck," Uncle Seth said. He knew how impatient Ma was, and how vexed she got when events didn't go off on time. It even happened with baby Marcy, who had been in no hurry to be born. Ma finally got tired of waiting and went off in the woods to the cabin of an old medicine woman—Choctaw, Uncle Seth said. She must have been good at her medicine because Ma took a potion of some kind and delivered baby Marcy that night.

Of course, baby Marcy was already *there*—she just happened to be inside rather than outside. The boat was different: it *wasn't* there.

"I expect it'll show up within the next few minutes," Uncle Seth said, uneasily.

"He's a cheerful one, ain't he?" Aunt Rosie said. "My bet would be that it never shows up."

"Of course it will—I paid our passage," Uncle Seth said.

"All of it?" Ma asked.

"No—I ain't a fool. Half of it," he said.

"Neva, go ask the Indian gentleman if he's seen a boat," Ma said.

"A flatboat," Uncle Seth said. "It had a fence around the deck to keep the animals from jumping off."

I was shy around strangers, and Neva wasn't, which is why Ma asked her to go quiz the Indian. Even so, my feelings were hurt—I *was* the oldest, and it should have been my job. But Neva trotted right down to the Indian, a medium-sized man.

Probably it was his canoe pulled up on the bank. Neva asked her question and the man, who had finally got his line untangled, listened to her patiently. When Neva came back he followed, a step or two behind her.

"It burnt—that's that," Neva said. "I guess we'll have to go back home."

"I thought Seth was being too cheerful," Aunt Rosie said.

Sally, Uncle Seth's mare, whinnied again, and Mr. Hickok came loping up.

"Here's Bill—I guess he finished his toddy," Uncle Seth said.

"Why hello, Charlie, hoping for a perch for breakfast?" Mr. Hickok said, speaking to the Indian man. He tipped his hat to Ma and Aunt Rosie.

"I may find a fish a little later," the man said. "Right now I was going to explain to these people that the boat they were expecting burned last night. I think all the people on it made it to shore. I was passing and helped two of them who were tired of swimming."

"Damn the luck!" Ma said. I had never heard her curse before.

"Yes, it was bad luck," the Indian said politely.

"You could introduce us, Bill, since it seems this gentleman and you are friends," Uncle Seth said, in an amiable tone. I believe, with Ma so angry, he was glad of the company.

"Oh, ain't you met?" Mr. Hickok said. "This is Charlie Seven Days, of the Lemhi people, from up near the Snake River, I believe—Charlie's a far piece from home."

"What people?" Uncle Seth asked, stepping down from the wagon seat.

"Lemhi—Shoshone," the man said in a careful tone, nodding to us all.

"I've heard of the Snake River, but it's out of my territory—so far, at least," Uncle Seth said.

"Charlie has the knack of turning up just when you need him," Mr. Hickok said. "He got me across a patch of thin ice once, during the war, and if he hadn't, I believe the Rebs would have caught me."

"Well, if he had a boat, we'd need him," Ma said. "We can't all fit in that canoe."

"Seen any boats, in your travels?" Uncle Seth asked.

"There is a steamboat tied up at Glasgow, which is not too far, but I don't know if it is a good boat, or if you could hire it," the Indian said.

Glasgow was several miles up the river—if we were going to take our wagon across the plains we ought to at least be able to take it that far.

"What brought you this far south?" Mr. Hickok inquired. "I thought you usually favored the northern climes."

"The Old Woman sent me to find her son," Charlie Seven Days said. "She thought he might be in St. Louis—but he's not in St. Louis. I think he may be in California, but I'm not sure. Now I have to go back and tell her he is still lost."

"What's he talking about?" Uncle Seth asked. "What old woman?"

"The Old One—the one who went with the first captains," Charlie said.

"Lewis and Clark, the woman who went with them—I forget her name," Mr. Hickok said. "I believe she lives on the Snake River somewhere, which is where Charlie's from."

"Is that in the direction of Wyoming?" Ma asked.

"Yes," Charlie said.

"Then you're going the same direction we are," Ma said. "Why don't you come with us? I'd feel more comfortable if we had a guide who knew the country."

That proposition didn't seem to surprise Charlie Seven Days, but it sure surprised Uncle Seth.

"A guide?" he said. "What do you think I am, if not a guide?"

"My brother-in-law," Ma said.

"But we just met this fellow," Uncle Seth said. "He may have plans of his own."

Ma's proposition didn't seem to faze Charlie Seven Days at all.

"I could take you as far as South Pass," he said. "That is where I must go north, to find the Old Woman. She is afraid her son might have died."

"What do we do about your canoe?" Ma asked Mr. Seven Days.

"We could just go back to the cabin and wait until the next good flatboat shows up," Uncle Seth said. I don't think he liked the quick way Ma took to Charlie Seven Days.

"No," Ma said. "We left. We're gone. I'm not going back. If I have to drive this wagon every step of the way to Wyoming, then I will."

Charlie Seven Days was considering the question of his canoe, which sure wouldn't fit in our wagon.

"I don't want to leave this canoe," Charlie said. "We might need it up the river—sometimes the big boats get stuck. I will paddle up to Glasgow and meet you there—it's only a day, for you, if you travel steady."

"You don't have to worry about the steady travel," Uncle Seth said. "If there's one thing I know about Mary Margaret, it's that once she starts traveling she'll travel steady."

"Getting her to stop long enough for my naps, that'll be the problem," Granpa said.

"I ain't able to sleep sound in a moving wagon," he added.

"I will meet you at the dock in Glasgow," Charlie said. "You should be there about sundown."

Then he got in his canoe and paddled away.

"This is your doing, Bill," Uncle Seth said, still exercised about Ma's decision. "Now we're saddled with an Indian we don't know a thing about."

Mr. Hickok was not disturbed.

"Seth, I done you a favor—there's no better man to travel with than Charlie," he said. "They say he knows every creek and varmint den in the west, and I believe it."

"Thank you for your introduction, Mr. Hickok," Ma said. "We had better be on our way now—I mean to make Glasgow by sundown."

Ma clucked, and the mules moved. In a minute

she had the wagon turned and we were on the north road. As we passed Mr. Hickok he tipped his hat three times, once to Ma, once to Aunt Rosie, and even once to Neva, who blushed when he done it.

"This departure is sure a heartbreaker for good old Boone's Lick," he said. "There'll be a drastic shortage of pretty ladies, now that the three of you are taking your leave."

"Well, Bill, at least you got a horse," Aunt Rosie said. "I guess you can just ride off yourself, if you're so lonesome."

**17** I DOUBT we'll ever see that Indian again," Uncle Seth said, when we were a mile or two up the north road.

Nobody answered him.

"He may have fooled Bill Hickok but he didn't fool me," he went on. "I suspect that story about the boat burning, too. That boat was floating on water—they could have just splashed water on it, if it was afire. For all we know this Charlie Seven Days could have massacred the boatmen—that boat's probably drifting down toward St. Louis now, with everybody on it scalped."

"I didn't see a knife," Aunt Rosie said.

"Oh, an Indian's always got a knife about him somewhere," Uncle Seth said. "Mary Margaret, I wish you'd let me drive these mules."

Ma wouldn't, though. She just ignored Uncle Seth, and when Granpa Crackenthorpe tried to get her to stop the wagon under a shade tree for a few minutes, so he could nap without being jostled, she ignored him too.

"We'll never get to Wyoming if we stop all the time," she said. "What's the matter with you, G.T.?"

He had been looking down in the mouth all day—I think leaving home had upset him.

"He's homesick, the oaf!" Neva said.

G.T. tried to slug her—they tussled for a while. G.T. was having to sniff back tears.

"I didn't know you were such a homebody, G.T.," Aunt Rosie said.

"Didn't neither," G.T. said, still sniffing.

"Well, if I ain't even gonna be trusted to drive the team there's no reason for me to bounce along in such a rude conveyance," Uncle Seth said.

He jumped down, unhitched his gray mare, and rode off.

"You're too rough on Seth," Aunt Rosie said, to Ma.

"Think so? I don't," Ma said.

Actually I agreed with Aunt Rosie. Ma was real short-tempered with Uncle Seth—we all noticed it.

"I hope Seth comes back, but I don't know why he would, the way you treat him," Granpa said. "A brother-in-law will only put up with so much at the hands of a woman."

We left the docks in Boone's Lick not long after sunup, but the sun just kept on climbing. Soon it was right overhead. Aunt Rosie handed Marcy to

Ma, who nursed her while we were clipping along—not fast, of course, but steady.

"When do the rest of us get to eat?" G.T. asked—he was still looking low.

"I'll feed you," Aunt Rosie said, since Ma had her hands full with the mules and the baby. A little horse meat jerky and a spud was all we got.

By then Uncle Seth had been gone three hours and there was no sign of him. The north road passed some pretty heavy woods, a fact which made G.T. nervous.

"There could be a whole crowd of bears in woods that thick," he commented. He was squeezing his rifle hard, as if it were a live thing that might slip away.

I didn't care for thick woods either, though it was bandits I mostly worried about. Several people had been robbed on the Glasgow road—if some of the Millers came at us I didn't know what I would do. Mule travel was monotonous, though. Despite his need not to be jostled when he slept, Granpa Crackenthorpe was sound asleep, snoring his scratchy snore. Aunt Rosie was nodding too. Neva crawled up by Ma, who let her drive the team for a mile or two, while she nursed the baby a second time. That struck me as unfair.

"I guess *I* can drive a team," I said, to remind them that I was still the oldest boy.

"I know that, but right now I'm training your sister," Ma said. "You're the lookout—I'm counting on you to warn me if you see anything out of the ordinary."

Ma had barely finished appointing me lookout when I saw something pretty out of the ordinary: a large man with a frizzy beard nearly down to his waist was sitting on a stump by the road. He was dressed in a brown robe, like priests wear, and was trying to get a sticker or something out of one foot. So far as I could tell he was barefooted—I didn't see any shoes. In fact I didn't see any kind of satchel or bag anywhere or anything: the man was just carrying himself. He wasn't quite as old as Granpa, but he wasn't young either.

"I wouldn't want to box that old priest," G.T. said. "He's big."

I was hoping Ma would clip on by, in case the man was a bandit disguised as a priest, but Ma didn't seem worried about that possibility. She stopped the wagon.

"Are you injured, Father?" she asked.

"Tacks," the priest said. "Some careless soul has spilled tacks in the public road and I stepped right in them. Is that Hubert Crackenthorpe sitting there snoring? I have not seen Hubert since the troubles on the Bad Axe River, which occurred thirty-four years ago last month. I was young then. I had been ministering to the Sauks, but after the massacre there were not many Sauks left to minister to. I had just come from France and spoke little English. In fact I mastered Sauk and a little Ioway before I ever learned English. My great-grandfather invented the algebra, although he didn't get the credit."

He stood up and carefully put four or five tacks in a pocket of his robe—the tacks he had taken out of his foot seemed to be his only equipment.

"We're on our way to Glasgow to look for a boat," Ma said. "You're welcome to get in and ride, since you've hurt your foot. Pa will be glad to see an old friend, when he wakes up."

The priest looked up the north road toward Glasgow before accepting Ma's offer.

"I have taken a vow to walk the earth, but I guess a wagon seat is not too far above the earth," he said. He was so big that when he hoisted himself up, the whole wagon tipped.

"I can jump down if I see a soul that needs ministering to," he said.

The solemn way he said it tickled Aunt Rosie, who laughed.

"If all you're looking for is souls that need mending you don't have to jump down," she said. "There are several right here in this wagon that could use a little mending."

"Oh my Lord, it's Père Villy!" Granpa said—he had just woke up.

The priest reached back a big hand and gave Granpa a good handshake. Granpa was so excited he was ready to jump up and down.

"Where are you bound for, Villy?" he asked.

"I'm on my way to Siberia," the priest said, as if he were talking about a place we would all be familiar with.

"Is that farther than Omaha?" Neva asked. She was now squeezed in between the big priest and Ma, but she still had the reins to the team.

The priest's chuckle seemed to come out of the

depths of his belly—it was like a sound made far underground.

"Much farther than Omaha, young miss," the priest said. "Siberia is part of Russia, which is across the sea. I have decided to go minister to the wandering Koraks—they're still stuck in heathenism, I hear."

I believe that remark even surprised Ma, who is thoroughly hard to surprise. Even finding out that the elk she thought she shot was only a horse didn't surprise her much.

"But Father Villy, there's no ocean nearby," she pointed out.

Father Villy chuckled again. "I believe the Pacific is less than two thousand miles west," he said. "Possibly no more than seventeen hundred miles from the Missouri shore. I'm a steady walker—at least I am when I can avoid tacks."

"Villy ain't bragging," Granpa assured us. "He had already walked down from Quebec before we got in that scrape on the Bad Axe."

"I guess you could go on the riverboat with us— that is, if we have a riverboat when we get to Glasgow," Ma said.

G.T. and I exchanged looks—even Neva threw back a glance. What was Uncle Seth going to think now? Ma had already invited an Indian to make the trip with us, and now she was inviting a priest.

"You're a kind woman, *madame*," the priest said. "I would enjoy a boat trip at least as far as the mouth of the Platte. Then I expect I had better walk the Holy Road."

"What Holy Road?" Aunt Rosie asked. "I didn't know there were *any* roads in that part of the country."

"Some call it the Oregon Trail," the priest said. "But the native peoples, which would be the Sioux and the Cheyenne, and the Shoshone, Pawnee, Arapaho, and a few others, call it the Holy Road. So many immigrants have moved along it in the last few years that there's a fair track along the Platte."

"I've heard my husband say that," Ma said. "Have you met him, Father? Dick Cecil. He's a wagoneer."

"No, I haven't," the priest said. "But if he's a wagon-driving man you'll probably find him in Wyoming. They've put up three new forts, which is foolish—I don't think the Indians will tolerate it— but there's plenty of work for wagoners in that part of the country, servicing those forts."

"Good—I need to find Dick Cecil quick," Ma said. "Introduce yourselves to the father, children—and you too, Rosie. If we're going to be traveling together we need to get the names straight."

When the big priest smiled it was like sunlight shining through a haystack: his whole beard moved, and he had a lot of beard. We all said our names, and Rosie held up baby Marcy, who immediately grabbed a fistful of that beard. Marcy didn't want to turn loose, either—Rosie had to pry her fingers off it.

"My name is Emile Villegagnon," the priest said, rolling the sound out. "That's easy for a Frenchman,

but I've found it's too much for the American tongue
so I'm just Père Villy to most people."

"Smart thinking," Granpa said. "A man could
choke himself trying to say a name like yours."

G.T. and Neva and I were nervous about what
Uncle Seth would think when he came back to the
wagon and saw a big priest with a brown robe sitting on the wagon seat beside Ma. Uncle Seth was
apt to get testy when he wasn't allowed to control
the planning, and Ma sure hadn't allowed him to
control much of it lately. She had already tacked
two people on to the expedition without so much as
a fare-you-well, and we had only been gone from
Boone's Lick part of one day.

In spite of his vow to walk the earth Father Villy
sat on the wagon seat and chatted with Ma the whole
afternoon. The rocking of the wagon was so restful
that I dozed, much of the time. If anybody kept a
lookout it was G.T., who still had bears on his mind.

"I think you may have run Seth off for good,"
Aunt Rosie said, as we were pulling into Glasgow—
most of the town was on a bluff, with the dock
down below, on the river.

"Who is Seth?" the priest asked.

"Her brother-in-law. She just run him off with
her sass," Granpa informed him. He seemed to be
more and more set against Ma—maybe it was because she wouldn't stop for his naps.

"I expect Seth will be at the docks, waiting for
us," Ma said. "I hope Mr. Seven Days is with him."

"You wouldn't be speaking of Charlie Seven
Days, would you?" the priest asked.

"Why, yes—we met him this morning," Ma said. "I asked him to come with us. Do you know him?"

"Since he was a boy," Father Villy said. "I taught him his letters, in a little school I ran for a while up at Fort Union—that's where the Yellowstone River comes into the Missouri."

"I would as soon swallow ice as wade in the Yellowstone," Granpa said. "They say it's a mighty cold river."

"Chill, yes," Father Villy said. "The fact is I gave Charlie his name. When I explained that the Lord made the world in six days and rested on the seventh he decided to call himself Charlie Seven Days. He has a Shoshone name too, of course, but that one's even harder on the tongue than mine. I think it had something to do with the sound a beaver makes when it slaps its tail on the water. It's a sound you won't hear too often now. They've about trapped out the beaver."

By the time we came to the docks the sun seemed to be setting right into the river, upstream where it curved to the west.

"I hear fiddling, and some fool's blowing on a jug," Granpa said.

Granpa Crackenthorpe was right, for once. There was a flatboat tied up at the docks, with several jolly boatmen doing a dance on the deck. Besides the fiddle and the jug, a skinny man was playing the Jew's harp. Uncle Seth was dancing on deck, too— Charlie Seven Days, who wasn't on deck, was holding Sally, Uncle Seth's mare. Father Villy jumped off the wagon and went to talk to his old pupil, who didn't seem a bit surprised to see him.

Ma was watching Uncle Seth dance on the river-boat.

"Drunk—he's missing his steps," Ma said. "You fools who thought I ran him off don't know Seth like I do. I couldn't run him off if I tried."

To my astonishment, before the wagon was even fully stopped, Ma put me in charge of the mules and skipped up on deck herself, to dance with Uncle Seth. Aunt Rosie looked a little pouty at that development.

"Mary Margaret has always got her way—except maybe with Dick," she said.

It wasn't a minute later that she stuck Marcy in my arms and jumped down herself—before you could say Jack Sprat she was on deck too, dancing with Father Villy. For a big man who had stepped on tacks earlier in the day he seemed to be light on his feet. After the first fiddler quit—to cut himself a chaw of tobacco—Granpa saw his chance and began to saw away on *his* fiddle. Next thing I knew the dancers had switched partners—Ma was dancing with the priest and Aunt Rosie with Uncle Seth.

G.T. saw a big snapping turtle resting on the bank and decided to go and harass it—G.T. hated snapping turtles. But then Charlie Seven Days strolled over and persuaded him to leave it alone. He talked to the big turtle as if it were a dog and the snapper picked itself up and waddled back into the river.

In a while the moon came up and made the water silvery. Neva had jumped on the boat by this time—she was dancing with herself. If Uncle Seth was drunk, *I* couldn't tell it: he and Ma were swirling all over the deck. Aunt Rosie and Father Villy weren't doing badly, either.

The only people left in the wagon were Marcy and myself—and Marcy didn't particularly like me. She had a sullen look on her face, as if she were just daring me to do something that would make her cry. I would have liked to be on the boat with the dancers. Uncle Seth had worn out, but not Ma—she was dancing with one of the boatmen. But I knew it was my duty to stay with the mules.

Uncle Seth finally saw me in the wagon, looking left out, because he strolled over and took Marcy, who immediately began to bubble and coo.

"Go stomp around a little, Shay, before the fiddlers wear out," he said. "I'll tote this baby for a while."

Aunt Rosie grabbed my arm the minute I stepped onto the boat, and danced with me until the fiddlers quit. I got my feet tangled up two or three times, which just made her chuckle.

"I don't know that you're going to be much of a ladies' man, Shay," she said. "That's what I like about you."

The jug man and the skinny fellow with the Jew's harp quit; they walked off up the hill toward town. The first fiddler played a few more tunes with Granpa, who was just getting warmed up. It did him no good—the dancers were mostly beginning to flag. Ma walked over and had a little discussion with Uncle Seth. Aunt Rosie sat on deck, fanning herself. Father Villy was cooling his feet in the river.

Neva wouldn't stop dancing, although the only musician left was Granpa and he was a scratchy fiddler. Neva wanted me to jog with her, but my feet had begun to feel like I had lead in my socks.

I had lived on the Missouri River all my life, and I liked having it near—only then it had just been a part of home, and now it wasn't, anymore. Pretty as it was, with the moonlight shining on it, it had stopped seeming like our old friendly river. Uncle Seth told me it was more than two thousand miles long, which was a lot more miles than I could imagine. A river that ran on for such a stretch could easily swallow a little wagon full of Cecils.

Ma knew that I was prone to glooms—thick, heavy glooms that settled on me and slowed me down so that I had a hard time moving, or thinking, or doing much of anything. When she saw me standing on the deck of the boat, something about the way I looked or the way I stood must have told her one of my glooms had come on me.

"Sherman, come here," she said—it was only at such times that Ma called me by my full name.

It made G.T. jealous, because she never called him by his full name, which was Grant Thaddeus Cecil.

"You're homesick, I guess," Ma said, once we had walked a little way down the riverbank, out of the hearing of the others.

I *was* homesick, but my feelings were so mixed that I couldn't find words for them— I don't think Ma even expected me to. She rubbed my neck and tried to hug me, but I stepped away. Even though I was glad Ma called me over, I didn't want anybody hugging me, just then.

"Sherman, would you just give it a chance?" Ma asked. "Wyoming might be a fine place to live, for all you know."

Then baby Marcy began to holler—Uncle Seth couldn't soothe her, and neither could Aunt Rosie.

"She's hungry—she wants the teat," Ma said. "That's one thing I've never been shut of for long—hungry babies."

"That Indian Charlie can talk to snapping turtles and have them mind him," G.T. said. He had seen Ma walk off with me—of course, it made him jealous, immediately.

"Was he talking to it in Indian language, or in turtle language?" Ma asked, before walking off to nurse Marcy.

"What do you think, Shay?" G.T. asked. The question had not occurred to him.

"I expect it was Indian language," I said, taking a guess. "I don't think turtles have a language."

"Maybe not, but they can listen," G.T. said. "That one was listening to every word Charlie said."

Pretty soon Uncle Seth took his horse and all the mules up the street to the town—he was hoping to find a livery stable. Aunt Rosie went with him. I imagine both of them were *really* hoping to find a saloon.

The rest of us made pallets under the wagon and soon bedded down. Father Villy slept with us—he had a snore that made Granpa's seem like a birdsong. I believe Charlie Seven Days slept in his canoe, which was tied up by the big flatboat.

The next morning, as soon as there was a shading of light in the east, the boatmen began to rattle around in on the boat, determined to get an early start. Cocks were crowing, up on the hill where the town was. It was so misty for half an hour that I couldn't see Aunt Rosie or Uncle Seth, but I heard some wild geese honking, high overhead, and a bull bellowed from somewhere way upstream.

"It's a bear, I can hear it plain," G.T. insisted.

"You oaf, it's a bull," Neva said, and for once she was right.

Ma routed us out—the priest too—and pretty soon we had the mules hitched and the wagon solidly settled on the flatboat, with a chain around the axle and chunks of wood under the wheels to keep it from rolling around.

A few minutes after sunup we left the Glasgow shore: Ma and Uncle Seth, Aunt Rosie and Granpa Crackenthorpe, me and G.T. and Neva and baby Marcy, big-bearded Father Villy and Charlie Seven Days, the man who could talk to turtles and whose real name meant the sound a beaver makes when it slaps its tail on the water.

It was good-bye to Missouri—I didn't know if we'd ever be back.

# BOOK II
# The Holy Road

**1** I EXPECT one reason most boat-men are stumpy little fellows is that there's no great amount of room on a boat. There were four boatmen on our boat, besides ourselves; when all was fine and fair, everybody lolled around on deck, fishing or playing cards or doing whatever they wanted to do. But it was not always fine and fair—we'd not been gone from Glasgow two hours when some clouds came scudding in, almost as low as a flight of ducks—big raindrops began to splatter down. There was a little shed of sorts, at one end of the boat, which was where we all huddled when the downpour came. The only travelers who didn't seek cover were Father Villy and Charlie Seven Days. Charlie stood on the edge of the deck with his shirt off—to him the rain was just a refreshing bath.

"I hope you have a better opinion of Mr. Seven Days now," Ma said, watching the rain splatter down. I believe she was bored by the lagging conversation, the result of the fact that Uncle Seth and Aunt Rosie had had a late night.

"I have no opinion of anything or anybody," Uncle Seth replied.

"Being surly is no way to start a trip, Seth," Ma said. She herself seemed to be in first-rate spirits.

"Well, I didn't expect it to cloud up so quick," Uncle Seth said.

"It's just a shower," Aunt Rosie said.

"Yes, but fish don't bite when it's this wet," one of the boatmen said, the skinny one who liked to play the Jew's harp. His name was Joe.

"Joe, that's erroneous," Uncle Seth said. "It's wet all the time for a fish, remember?"

"Go to hell, this ain't your boat!" Joe said. He was a testy little fellow.

While we all watched, Father Villy walked to the edge of the boat, stripped off his robe, stood there naked for a minute, and then dove in the water. Before we knew it he had swum all the way to the east bank.

"I guess a priest can just go naked when he wants to," Aunt Rosie said, a little shocked.

"Villy was always that way," Granpa said. "He shucks off when he feels like it."

"Do you like him, Seth?" Ma asked.

"Well, he's large—that could be useful if there's a fight," Uncle Seth said. "Another advantage is that he can marry people. On a long expedition like this somebody might get the itch to be hitched."

"It won't be me, if that's what you're thinking," Aunt Rosie said.

"A man Seth's age who has never been married doesn't know what he's talking about," Ma said.

Ma and Uncle Seth went on joshing and bickering, just as they would have if we'd been at home. Charlie Seven Days had just eased his canoe into the water—I walked over to watch.

"I am just going to look for snags and sandbars," he said. "You're welcome to come if you're not busy."

The problem of snags and sandbars is one boatmen have to deal with every day of their lives, if they happen to be on the Missouri River. Trees wash down and wedge themselves in the channel sometimes just below the surface. No boatman can spot them all, because looking into the Missouri is like looking into a cup of coffee—if not worse. Of course, Charlie couldn't see beneath the surface any better than anybody else, but he was quick to probe with his paddle if he suspected a snag, and more often than not he was right.

The shower soon blew on through, and a bright sun came out. The sky above the river got bigger and bigger and bluer and bluer. Birds of all sorts flitted around the water's edge—the sky above was thick with ducks and geese, one bunch flying right behind another. I stopped feeling homesick and began to feel lively. We were finally on our way upriver, headed for a big adventure.

While we were paddling along Father Villy came swimming back from the far shore. He swam beside the canoe for a while, flopping around in the water like a big hairy water animal.

"This water is nearly as muddy as mud," he said, as he swam away.

Charlie Seven Days began to teach me how to spot snags—it meant staying alert to little patterns of water.

"See that ripple?" Charlie said, pointing at a patch of water just upstream.

At first I *didn't* see the ripple. The surface of the river was never steady for long: there would always be little waves, or a fish would jump and go back down with a splash, or a waterbird would skim the surface and disturb the water. We had already seen several muskrats, but it didn't take a critter the size of a muskrat to disturb the water. Even a water bug could do it, skipping along. But, by looking close, I finally *did* see the ripple Charlie was talking about, just a little *V* where the water edged around something hidden just underneath it. Sure enough, when Charlie probed underneath it with his paddle, he struck a snag. I soon got so I could spot the ripples myself—I wasn't as expert at it as Charlie, of course, but I was sharp-eyed enough that I could save the boat from getting stuck, most times.

Sandbars were harder to spot, because the river just surged right over them, with no change the eye could spot.

"I keep a watch for cranes and herons," Charlie said. "They like to set down where the water is shallow."

On the west side of the river there would now and then be a good break in the trees—I could see stretches of brown prairie and was hoping any minute to spot my first buffalo, but when I asked Charlie about buffalo he shook his head.

"We will be lucky if we see buffalo," he said.

I was shocked. Pa and Uncle Seth had always talked about the great herds of buffalo that covered the prairies. They claimed a hunter could just stand at the edge of the herd and shoot as many as he wanted, and they bragged about how good buffalo liver tasted, and buffalo tongue. Uncle Seth even explained how he liked to sprinkle a little bile out of the spleen, to give the meat more flavor.

"But I thought there were millions of them," I said.

"Not along the Holy Road—not now," Charlie said. "Animals won't stay in places where too many people shoot at them."

When we got back to the boat I took the matter up with Uncle Seth, who looked a little hangdog.

"Charlie's right—they're scarce now—too many immigrants," he said. "I expect we'll scare up a few when we get to Wyoming, if that's where we're going."

Ma was washing clothes. One day on the river and she already felt the need of a big wash. The wet clothes were spread out on the roof of the little shed, drying. The boatmen, though they lived on the water, could not be described as clean and tidy. They looked at Ma as if she were crazy. Aunt Rosie was dozing in a little spot of shade, and Neva and G.T. were playing a dice game with the priest, using borrowed dice.

When Uncle Seth raised the question of where we were going, Ma sort of cocked her head.

"Where else would we be going, if not Wyoming?" she asked. "That's where they're building the new forts—where would Dick be, if not in Wyoming?"

Uncle Seth shrugged. "This west is a big place," he said. "Ideal for a wandering man. It's a long sail up to Fort Union—Dick could be anyplace."

"Fort Union, that's too north," Granpa said. "You're apt to need snowshoes, when you're that far north."

For some reason Ma wasn't satisfied with Uncle Seth's answer, though it seemed reasonable to me. Pa went where he wanted to—he had no fondness for carpentry and might shy away from fort building if he got the chance. Uncle Seth was right about one thing: the west was big. Already the sky looked bigger than the sky over Boone's Lick—and we hadn't even been going upriver a whole day.

Ma had a different reasoning process than most people. Answers that sounded fine to me or G.T. or even Neva didn't satisfy Ma.

"You know more than you're telling, don't you, Seth?" Ma said, staring at him. "You're Dick's partner—I expect you know where he is."

"Why would I? It's been fourteen months since I set eyes on Dick Cecil," Uncle Seth said. The red vein popped out on his nose, a sign that he was nervous, or might be getting mad.

Ma didn't press him—not in words—but it was plain that she had a suspicion. Uncle Seth stood up, had a stretch, and went over and began a conversation with Charlie Seven Days.

That was the end of the talk about Wyoming for that day.

**2** T H E   boatmen were afraid to travel on the river after dark. Even Charlie Seven Days couldn't spot snags in the dark. So when evening came the boatmen tied up on the bank. We stopped about an hour before dark, to give our hunters—Uncle Seth and Charlie—a chance to rustle up some game. Uncle Seth saddled Sally and headed due west, while Charlie strolled off toward a little grove of trees a mile or two from the riverbank. G.T. was annoyed, because he wasn't allowed to hunt.

"Fish, if you want to do something useful," Ma told him.

"Why? I'm a poor fisherman and you know it," G.T. said, in a sassy tone. Two minutes later he landed a twenty-pound catfish.

"I guess it's a good thing you're a poor fisherman," Ma said. "If you were a good fisherman you might have caught one so big it would tip the boat."

G.T. just stared at the fish, as if he could hardly believe he'd caught it.

It turned out to be a lucky day for hunters *and* fishermen. Uncle Seth came back in half an hour with a fat little doe across his Sally's rump, and Charlie walked in a few minutes later with two wild turkeys.

Father Villy turned out to be a big help with the cooking. Ma wouldn't usually allow anyone to interfere with her when she was cooking, but she made an exception for Father Villy and he concocted a kind of sweetbreads stew which we all thought was tasty.

"I cooked for the garrison up at Fort Pierre," he said. "The real cook died of jaundice. I have never seen a human being turn so yellow."

"He must have overdone the rum—it'll turn a person yellow," Uncle Seth volunteered.

"No, I'm afraid it was witchcraft," the priest said. "There was an Arapaho medicine man who took against him and made a spell that turned him yellow."

"I know that medicine man," Charlie said. "He calls himself the Man of the Morning."

"That's him, the rascal," Father Villy said.

"Why, I believe I've seen him too," Uncle Seth said. "He was around Fort Laramie for a while— Dick and I even gave him a ride once or twice. I've heard he poisons people with cactus buds."

Uncle Seth and Father Villy went on talking about the bad medicine man who turned people yellow, but Charlie took his plate and went over to the edge of the boat to eat. He was a man who seemed to live in his own space—sometimes he would invite you into it, but sometimes not. When he finished his sweetbreads he washed his plate in the river.

Ma was sitting outside the little shed, nursing Marcy and thinking her own thoughts, the way she did. It was not smart to barge into Ma's space, either, when she was thinking her own thoughts—she was like Charlie in that way.

What got me was how the priest and Uncle Seth and Charlie Seven Days seemed to know just about everybody there was to know, up and down the plains. From what I had heard, the west was such a huge place that you'd be lucky to meet ten people a month, but Uncle Seth and the priest and Charlie soon discovered that they had several acquaintances in common—for all the big space, there were just so many forts, where the old-timers and the newcomers mixed and mingled.

I was anxious to get to one of the forts myself. I wanted to meet some of the famous mountain men—Jim Bridger, Kit Carson, and the like: the men Uncle Seth was always telling stories about.

That night I had a dream about Henry Clay, our mule that the Millers and the Tebbits had skinned and eaten. I was riding Henry Clay along at a brisk clip, and we seemed to be going to a fair or something, because I could hear music in the distance, but we never quite got to the fair. Somehow we missed it and ended up back in our old freight yard—already half the pens had been knocked down, and the cabin had begun to sag in.

I was dozing on deck when I had this dream— the next thing I knew, Ma had hold of me and was trying to drag me under the shed. A wild storm had come up—the river was pitching the boat around like a chip. Lightning flashed like white fire and in the flash I saw Little Nicky, the mule, get thrown clear over the edge into the river. For a while the lightning was so bad that I kept my eyes squeezed shut, to protect my eyeballs. Uncle Seth and Charlie Seven Days were struggling to keep any more of the animals from pitching overboard. While they were hanging on to the livestock the little shed blew clean away, into the river somewhere behind us. There was nothing we could do except huddle together and wait out the storm. At one point the boat gave such a lurch that baby Marcy popped out of Ma's arms—luckily Aunt Rosie caught her. Of course, Marcy was screaming her lungs out, but we could only hear her for a second, between thunderclaps. In my mind I was still half in my dream, but the rest of me was wet as a dog, and cold.

It must have been nearly dawn when the storm struck, because lightning was still flashing to the east when the sky began to get red with the sunrise. For a few minutes clouds and thunder and sun all mixed together, but then the thunder became only a faint rumble, off in the distance, and the sun came up, round and warm.

"Count up," Ma said. "Some of us might be missing."

"I don't see Seth," Aunt Rosie said. "I don't see that skinny boatman, or Mr. Seven Days either."

"If we've lost Seth we're in for it," Ma said.

But we hadn't lost him—he had floundered ashore somehow and came walking along the riverbank, leading Little Nicky by his lead rope. We hadn't lost Joe, the skinny boatman, or Charlie Seven Days either—they had just gone off to fix a line to the little shed before it floated all the way down to the Mississippi. Uncle Seth finally had to unload all the mules and hitch them to that shed, in order to get it back upstream to the boat—it was then that I realized how powerful a river can be, when it's got something in its channel.

"These are just the pleasures of travel, I guess," Uncle Seth said, when he climbed back on deck. We were all still soaking wet.

"If you think this is pleasure, then I'd say you're a fool," Ma said. Sometimes she liked Uncle Seth's little jokes, and sometimes she didn't.

"But where is your old one?" Charlie asked, once he had his canoe safely back in place. "I don't see him."

Father Villy had been in the water, pulling with the mules, but he jumped back on deck quick enough, when he discovered we couldn't locate Granpa.

The fact was, Granpa Crackenthorpe was gone. There was not a trace of him to be seen.

"I should have tied him to something—I was so

scared for Marcy that I forgot him," Ma said, when it was clear that Granpa was gone. G.T. and Neva, neither of whom had ever liked Granpa, were bawling their heads off anyway.

"No, you don't want to tie somebody to a boat that's pitching," Uncle Seth said. He tried to put his arm around Ma but she shook him off. "A pitching boat can flip over, and then whoever's tied to it will be drownt for sure."

Ma didn't bother to answer him.

Of course, a storm that could pitch a full-grown mule overboard would have no trouble tossing a skinny old man.

Uncle Seth got back on Sally, and Charlie Seven Days untied his canoe. Father Villy walked down one bank of the river crying, "Hubert! Hubert!" at the top of his lungs, and then swam across and did the same on the other bank, all to no avail. No trace of Granpa was found.

I couldn't hold back the tears myself. Granpa Crackenthorpe had lived with us every day of my life. He wasn't especially agreeable, but on the other hand, there was no reason to stab him with a pocketknife, as G.T. had once done.

Uncle Seth and Charlie and Father Villy searched the river nearly all that day. Ma didn't help and didn't look—she sat at the stern of the boat, dry-eyed, leaving Marcy to Aunt Rosie's care, except when she needed to nurse.

The boatmen grew impatient. Once they got their flimsy shed nailed back on they wanted to be on their way upriver, but Uncle Seth insisted we wait.

"If Hubert managed to get loose from that big pistol of his, then he would have been light as a leaf," Uncle Seth said. "He could be ten miles downstream, wandering around in the mud, cussing us all."

Ma didn't answer. None of us were hungry that night. The boatmen ate most of what was left of the turkeys and the deer.

**3** W E searched downriver—all of us— for another whole day, but we didn't find Granpa. The boatmen grew so surly that Uncle Seth raised a temper and threatened to shoot all of them.

"Learn a little patience!" he said, with the vein popping on his nose.

"I fault myself for this," Ma said. "I should have left the bunch of you in Boone's Lick and gone looking for Dick myself."

"Mary, you've got a nursing baby," Uncle Seth reminded her. "You can't just go off and leave a nursing baby."

"I could—she's had about enough of the teat," Ma said. "Besides, there are nanny goats. Their milk is richer than mine."

Father Villy, like Ma, was cast into sadness by the loss of Granpa Crackenthorpe.

"Hubert survived the battle of the Bad Axe, which was so terrible that the Mississippi River ran red," Father Villy said. "Then a little freshet blew him away."

We were all willing to keep looking, but Ma shook her head.

"Time to give it up," she said—then she sat all day in the stern of the boat, alone with her thoughts.

The next morning the surface of the river was as smooth as if wind had never ruffled it. There was frost on the ropes we used to tie up the boat, and little crinkles of ice in the shallows along the shore. All day ducks came slanting in—sometimes there were a thousand or more of them on the river at once; their gabbling kept me awake and fear of storms kept G.T. awake. He had stopped worrying about bears and started worrying about dangerous clouds. Despite what Uncle Seth said about boats flipping over, G.T. tied himself to the railing every night, in a fearful mood.

After the fat doe, the turkeys, and the big catfish we all had high expectations for the hunt, but they were soon disappointed. Uncle Seth hunted much of the day, and Charlie Seven Days did too, but they brought home nothing. Charlie finally managed to snare a goose, but one goose didn't go far on a boat full of hungry people. Uncle Seth and Aunt Rosie went ashore in Westport and came back drunk, but Uncle Seth *had* managed to secure a ten-gauge shotgun and some duck shot. After that he and Charlie would float off into the mists that covered the river just before dawn. Sometimes they would catch a raft of ducks dozing together and kill thirty or forty of them with a single shot. We ate duck until we all got tired of the rubbery taste.

Once I did persuade G.T. to go for a hunt with me on the Kansas bank. Almost at once we spotted something that looked like a buffalo, far off in the grass.

"We'll be heroes if we kill it," G.T. said. We stalked that buffalo for over an hour, without getting much closer to it—our eyes weren't accustomed to the distances you found on the Kansas plains. The prairies looked flat, but had a slow roll to them, a kind of grassy wave.

Then the buffalo turned out to be nothing but a stray milk cow, a development that made G.T. furious.

"Let's kill it anyway," he said—of course I wouldn't let him.

"Heroes don't kill milk cows," I pointed out.

At close range the milk cow, which was brindle, looked more like a mule than a buffalo.

I turned around and started tramping back to the river, only to discover that G.T. thought the river was in the opposite direction.

"The river's this way," he insisted, pointing.

"You fool, it's *this* way, of course," I said.

The fact was, neither of us knew where the river was. The sun was hidden by some clouds as thick and gray as the grass we were walking on. There was not a single tree in sight, and no way to tell one direction from another. The harder we tried to choose a direction, the more confused we became. Instead of buffalo killers and heroes we were two lost hunters, with no idea how to get back to our boat.

"If the Blackfeet Indians show up they can scalp us pretty quick, I guess," G.T. said. The remark showed how little attention G.T. paid to what Uncle Seth said.

"The Blackfeet Indians live in Montana," I reminded him. "This is Kansas we're lost in."

"Maybe it is and maybe it isn't," G.T. said. He would never admit to being wrong.

"The boat's probably a hundred miles away by now," he said. "They'll never find us. We'll starve."

When G.T.'s spirits started to slide they usually slid a long way quick.

What saved us was that Ma had a cowbell. She thought we might acquire a milk cow, somewhere on our travels, so she packed our old cowbell. When she decided we were lost she began to ring it, and we could just hear that bell, ringing far to the east. It gave us a direction, and we started walking toward it. If Ma hadn't kept ringing the bell we would have probably drifted off line and been lost all night, but she kept ringing. Then Charlie Seven Days came walking out of the dusk and led us home.

"I guess we'll have to hobble you boys, if you can't manage your directions," Uncle Seth said.

That night I finally worked up to asking Charlie

a question I had been wanting to ask him since he decided to travel with us: it was about Ma mistaking a horse for an elk. I explained what Uncle Seth told me the Cheyenne would think, that the elk had been ready to die and just turned himself into a horse to help us out.

"Your uncle must think the Cheyenne are a foolish people," Charlie said. "What I think is that your mother needed to feed her family, and knew there was a lot of meat on that big horse."

"Then you don't think she really thought the horse was an elk?" I asked.

"A horse is not an elk," Charlie said. It was his final comment—I guess it might be that my mother was a liar after all.

**4** A s soon as Aunt Rosie got over her beating she began to pine for her old life. Her bruises cleared up and her split lip healed. Her ribs mended more slowly, but by the time we had edged upriver past St. Joseph and were close to White Cloud, she was well enough to bend over and lift a bucket of water out of the river.

It got colder as we traveled on into October. The ducks and geese were so noisy that sometimes we all wished Ma would unload the wagon and take us overland.

The day we were due to strike the Platte River Aunt Rosie came over to Ma and told her she wanted to get off and try life again on her own.

"I believe I'll try my luck in Council Bluffs," she said. "I've heard Iowa's nice."

"I don't agree with your decision," Ma said. She didn't say it angrily—she said it sadly.

"I got used to having my sister around again," she said.

Aunt Rosie looked sad herself, when Ma took that tone.

"I know, Mary Margaret," she said. "I've got used to having you, too. I've even got used to Seth, and he's a lot to get used to."

Uncle Seth didn't answer. He knew Rosie was just joshing.

"I need a town, Mary," Aunt Rosie said. "I'm no river girl and no country girl, either. I like a saloon with a piano—and maybe a few gentlemen callers."

"It was a gentleman caller who nearly beat you to death," Ma reminded her.

"No, that wasn't a gentleman caller—that was a sheriff," Rosie said. "Sheriffs are a hazard, particularly if there's a new preacher in town. But blizzards and wild Indians are hazards too."

"We didn't take you prisoner," Ma said. "We'll all miss your company, but you can go whenever you want."

We all felt sad, when we heard Ma's decision. We all loved Aunt Rosie, though we hadn't had her in our lives very long.

"Seth, what kind of town is Omaha?" Ma asked.

"Hilly," Uncle Seth said.

"I didn't mean that," Ma said. "You do irritate me sometimes, Seth."

"She means is there a sheriff there who is likely to beat me up?" Rosie said.

"I have not been there lately," Uncle Seth said. "It's just a town, filled with good men and bad, I expect. You might ask Villy—he's thoroughly informed."

Aunt Rosie walked off to quiz the priest. We all sat around, gloomy.

"I wish we'd never left home," Neva said.

"If we was home I'd probably catch a fine mess of crawdads, since it's fall," G.T. said, not that the comment made sense.

Before we could get even gloomier a fracas broke out among the boatmen. We all took Aunt Rosie's decision hard, but Joel, the shortest and skinniest of the boatmen, went wild when he heard she was leaving. Several of the boatmen were in love with Rosie, but Joel was so violently afflicted with love sentiments that he began to butt his head against the side of the boiler. We thought he'd surely stop, after two or three butts, but Joel didn't stop. Uncle Seth finally grew alarmed enough to intervene.

"Here now, son, don't do that," he said.

"I *will* do it!" Joel said. "I want to crack my head! I can't live without Rosie!"

We were all riveted by his effort to crack his skull against the boiler. Already his head was pretty bloody.

"Stop him, Seth!" Ma commanded.

It took Uncle Seth and Father Villy both to pull Joel away from the boiler, and then the minute they turned him loose he went racing right off the boat into the Missouri River.

"Then I'll drown!" he yelled.

We were tied up for the night—it was pitch dark when Joel went overboard. We heard one splash and then nothing—none of us could see a thing.

"That poor fellow's in the grip of a fit," Father Villy said.

"Yes, a love fit," Uncle Seth said. "I doubt we're rid of him, though. It takes determination to drown yourself in a river this shallow. I doubt he's got that much determination."

Uncle Seth was right. Joel slunk back on board a little later, shivering in his wet clothes.

The Platte River, which we came to the next day, looked just as muddy as the Missouri, but it wasn't as wide. There was no town to speak of, just a few shacks. A boat was stuck on a sandbar, a half mile or so up the Platte. The men who were struggling to pull it off looked like moving gobs of mud.

In the afternoon Ma told us to start packing the wagon, a tiresome chore. We had stuff scattered from one end of the boat to the other. Some of the utensils we had started out with must have been flung overboard, like Granpa. Many were never found, but we had a pretty full wagon anyway.

Aunt Rosie decided not to get off in Omaha—her intention was to stay on board until the boat reached Council Bluffs.

"What's wrong with Omaha?" Ma asked.

"The name—what does it mean?" Rosie asked.

"Oh, it's a tribe," Uncle Seth informed her. "I've met several Omahas."

"Well, it's not my tribe and besides, I've heard Iowa's pretty," Aunt Rosie said.

"Any place can be pretty if the sun's shining bright," Uncle Seth said.

Aunt Rosie's decision to stay on board a little longer made at least one person happy: Joel.

"I believe he thinks he can talk her into marriage between here and Council Bluffs," Uncle Seth said.

"I don't think he's aiming that high," Ma said. "But he is aiming."

Ma was tapping her fingers on the railing of the boat. It was a habit she had—she tapped her fingers when she was trying to make up her mind. Father Villy and Charlie Seven Days were planning to get off at the Omaha docks, but none of us knew for sure what Ma was planning.

"All right, Seth," she said suddenly. "What's the verdict? Do we get off here, or do we go on upriver?"

I had never seen Ma look at Uncle Seth quite as hard as she looked at him then. If her eyes had been nails he would have been nailed tight to the boat.

"It's your trip, Mary Margaret—why should I be the one to say?" he replied.

At that point people sort of melted back, toward the far side of the boat—all except me. I wanted to know what it meant that my mother was looking at my uncle that hard.

"Because you know where Dick is," Ma said. "Or if you don't know exactly, you can get us in the neighborhood."

"How would I?" Uncle Seth countered. "I ain't seen Dick in fourteen months—he could be anywhere."

But he seemed nervous, which wasn't his usual

way at all. Usually Uncle Seth's words just flowed right out and kept flowing.

"Because you'd know if he had a woman—an Indian woman," Ma said.

Everybody melted farther away—but Ma wasn't whispering, and I expect they heard.

"You better not play me false, Seth," Ma said. "I need to know where Dick Cecil is. I've already lost my own father because of this. Don't you play me false."

There was a silence so long and so tense that I considered just jumping in the river, like Joel had. Ma had Uncle Seth pinned to the deck with her eyes. He was going to have to answer her—there was no escape.

Aunt Rosie couldn't stand the strain.

"Just tell her, Seth," she said. "My Lord, she's his wife."

Just then we eased up to the Omaha docks, and Uncle Seth answered Ma's question by deciding to get us off the boat.

"Let's get this wagon off the boat," he said. "Sherman, you take charge of the extra mules. October's a fine time of year to be traveling on the Platte. If we travel steady I believe we can make the new forts by Christmas."

In only minutes we had the wagon and the livestock unloaded. Father Villy helped, plodding through the mud barefooted. Charlie planned to sell his canoe and buy a horse—he said he would meet us by nightfall.

When it came time to say good-bye to Aunt

Rosie, she cried, Ma cried, we children cried, baby Marcy cried, and the boatmen cried, even though she wasn't leaving *them*. With so many of us crying the boatmen couldn't keep from joining in.

But Ma and Aunt Rosie hugged one another the longest—you could see that it was a pain for the sisters to part.

Finally Ma crawled up onto the wagon seat, clucked to the mules, and we were all soon slogging through the Omaha mud. Aunt Rosie waved and waved, and we all waved back. When we went over the first hill Aunt Rosie was talking to Joel—they were both just dots on the river.

Neva and I would have liked to spend some time in Omaha—we had never seen brick buildings before, and Omaha had plenty of them. G.T. was sulking for some reason. We did stop at a big general store long enough to get a few supplies and replace some of the utensils that had washed overboard. Uncle Seth bought G.T. and I good strong hunting knives—he said we would need them soon. Neva got a new bonnet, and we were each allowed a piece of sticky molasses candy. Uncle Seth wanted to buy Ma a lace shawl, but she just looked at him funny and said: "Lace? You want to buy me lace, when we're going into the wilderness? A suit of armor would be more useful."

"Well, there'll be balls and such," Uncle Seth said. I think his feelings were a little hurt by her refusal.

"Remember how you used to shine at balls, Mary Margaret?" he said.

I guess Ma did remember—she softened to him a little, when he said that.

"I was a girl then," she said. "It's been such a while since I was a girl, Seth."

"It don't mean you can't still shine," Uncle Seth said—but he didn't buy the shawl. Instead he bought several sacks, which puzzled me, because we didn't have anything to put in them.

Charlie Seven Days caught up with us just before sundown, which was a relief to Ma—she had come to put a lot of trust in Charlie's judgment. The little sorrel horse he had bought wasn't much taller than a big dog. This amused Uncle Seth no end.

"My God, Charlie, that horse ain't big enough to fart," he said.

"Seth, watch your talk," Ma said.

That night we made our first campfire in Nebraska, using driftwood we found along the Platte River. Father Villy sat up late, teaching Neva French songs, of which he knew a bunch. Uncle Seth would usually jump into any sing-along, but this time he didn't. All evening, while the fire crackled, he hardly said a word.

"The stars are brighter in Nebraska," G.T. said. "Some of those stars look as big as rocks."

Ma kept her eyes on Uncle Seth—I think she may have felt that she had been too hard on him. At one point she offered him more coffee, but he just shook his head. I think that tussle of wills, between the two of them, had fairly worn him out.

**5** I HAVEN'T seen a tree since Wednesday—nearly a week," Ma said. "I never expected to be in a place where I wouldn't see a tree in a week. It's spooking me, Seth."

It was spooking me too, and Neva and G.T. as well. When we first left Omaha there were plenty of trees along the Platte, but after ten days or so they began to thin out. Then we seemed to have passed the last one. All we could see in any direction were little round, bumpy hills, covered with brown grass. There were bushes and reeds along the Platte—but that was all. G.T. had yet to catch a single crawdad in it, or even a good-sized frog.

"Rest your mind, Mary Margaret," Uncle Seth said. "There are trees farther west.—plenty of them."

"How much farther west?" Ma wanted to know.

"Six weeks should put us in some good thick trees," Uncle Seth said. "Let's just plug along and get to Fort Laramie. Then we might need to study the maps."

"Do you think Dick will be there?" Ma asked.

"No, but that's where we can pick up some useful news," Uncle Seth said. "There's be somebody at Fort Laramie who can help locate just about anybody you might name."

Ma didn't press the matter. After her set-to with Uncle Seth in Omaha they had soon got back on good terms—better terms than they had been on for a while, we all thought. At night Ma and Uncle Seth would still be sitting by the fire together, talking, when the rest of us got too tired to stay awake.

That was how it had been at home, for most of our lives—the sound of the two of them talking was usually the last thing we heard before we went to sleep.

What they talked about so much, I never knew, but the sound of their two voices made a good sound to go to sleep by—soothing, like the sound of rain.

That night it came a hard frost—hard enough to freeze the Platte, not to mention those of us in the wagon. The ducks that had been paddling around on the river the day before were walking around on solid ice, quacking and complaining. That was the day we learned what the sacks were for, that Uncle Seth had bought in Omaha. He gave one to me, one to G.T., and one to Neva.

"Turds," he said. "Go gather them. I imagine you'll be finding cow turds mostly, with maybe a pile of horse pods now and then. I'll give a dime to anyone who finds a buffalo chip."

For ten days we'd been following an immigrant train—a large one, with more than one hundred wagons in it. Every time we topped a hill we would see it, way off ahead. Neva was wild to catch up with them—she thought there'd be boys to play with—but Ma made no effort to catch up.

"When winter's coming and you're in country without wood it's fine luck to be behind a wagon train that big," Uncle Seth said. "A train that size will spew out droppings all day long. You three get to be our turd gatherers. Fill up your sacks and we'll have a fine campfire tonight."

"You mean we're going to burn turds?" G.T. asked. "We never burned turds in Missouri."

"You oaf, that was because we had *wood,* in Missouri," Neva said.

"This hard freeze will make your task easy," Uncle Seth said. "The droppings will be froze hard."

He was right on that point. The three of us filled several sacks with frozen droppings, and it didn't even take us much of the day. Once when we were a good distance from the wagon we heard a gunshot, which scared us good, but it was only Charlie Seven Days, who had managed to stalk a little antelope.

Though it warmed up considerably during the day, the wind rose just before sunset and some rolling black clouds began to spit little pellets of sleet at us.

"Ow, it's like needles," G.T. said. That *was* what the sleet felt like.

"Get behind your mules," Uncle Seth advised. "Let them take the brunt of it."

We huddled up behind the mules and crowded as close to them as we could. When the moon finally came up and the sleet stopped, the plains had a white, icy look—yet Father Villy was still walking around barefoot, indifferent to the fact that he was walking on sleet.

I don't think G.T. really believed that cow turds would burn, but they did. The priest and Uncle Seth banked the fire so skillfully that we were soon as warm as if we were burning wood.

Ma cooked part of Charlie's antelope, which was very tasty, but there was not much singing around the campfire that night. The hard freeze and the sleet reminded us that we were out in the middle of a bald plain, with no shelter except a wagon—and there was colder weather still to come.

"I wish you'd left me at home, Ma," G.T. said. "It's too chilly out here."

"Don't be a complainer," Ma said mildly. "You're safer with us than you would be at home."

"I guess I won't be, when the Indians come and cut off my ears," G.T. said.

"You oaf, why would they want your dirty ears?" Neva asked.

"Neva, stop calling him an oaf every minute," Ma said. "It's grating on my nerves."

"Mine too," I said—Neva gave me a black look.

What happened next reminded me of that day on

the river when G.T. said he was a poor fisherman
and then immediately landed a big catfish. He had
no sooner mentioned Indians when twenty or more
came riding over the nearest ridge, their horses
crunching the sleet under their hooves. We had
seen an Indian or two, as we came along the trail,
but to have twenty or more suddenly show up,
when we were alone on a frozen plain at night, was
such a shock that my hair stood up. G.T. was so
scared he couldn't close his mouth. Neva was the
opposite—she buttoned her lip. There were several
dogs traveling with the Indians, barking and howling: the sound carried far over the prairies.

All that saved us kids from panic was that none
of our men seemed alarmed. In fact, they didn't
even seem surprised, though they all did get to
their feet to greet the newcomers.

"I believe it's our Pawnee brethren," Father Villy
said. "I wondered when they'd be paying us a
visit."

"Do you speak the tongue, Charlie?" Uncle Seth
asked. "I have only a smattering, myself."

Charlie shook his head. He wasn't pleased to see
the Pawnees, but he wasn't scared, either.

Our menfolk may not have been scared, but our
mules were—either the smell of the Indian horses
or the howling of their dogs upset the mules
greatly. They were snorting and straining at their
ropes. Charlie and Uncle Seth went over to quiet
them down, while Father Villy and the rest of us
watched the Pawnees slip and slide down the sleety
ridge.

Ma had baby Marcy in her arms, wrapped up tight against the chill.

"There's no cause for alarm, ma'am," Father Villy assured her.

"I'm not alarmed," Ma said. "What do they want, barging in this time of night?"

Father Villy seemed startled that Ma would bring up the time.

"You'll not find too many red men who worry much about the time," he told Ma. "Time is just of a piece to them. They don't clock it apart, like we do."

"You'd think anybody could see it's bedtime," Ma said. "If those dogs don't quiet down they'll wake this baby."

"These Pawnee boys ain't hostile, but they're sly thieves," Father Villy said. "We need to guard our goods."

"Good advice," Uncle Seth said. "A quick Pawnee can steal the socks off a preacher—maybe that's why Villy goes barefoot. Probably lost so many socks he decided to give up on footware."

A minute later we had a passel of Indians crowding around us, horses snorting, dogs barking, the whole crowd smelling pretty rank. Four or five Indians tried to warm themselves by our fire, but most of them were eyeballing our equipment, crowding around the wagon and examining what they could find. Baby Marcy soon woke up and began to howl, a development that annoyed Ma.

Uncle Seth and Father Villy made an effort to be polite to the Pawnees, talking in sign to the skinny old fellow who seemed to be their headman. He

wore an old black hat and had a string of yellow bear teeth around his neck. He chattered away but I had no idea what he was saying. Meanwhile, Charlie planted himself by our horses and mules and kept a close watch on them.

"I've met this old rascal," Uncle Seth said. "He was at Fort Laramie for one of the big pows. His name is Nose Turns Down. His notion is that we should give him a mule."

"He won't get a mule, but he might get a piece of my mind if he doesn't get out of here and let us get some rest," Ma said.

An Indian came up to me and felt the buttons of my coat—another did the same to G.T., and one even pulled a comb out of Neva's hair. I guess he just wanted to look at it because he soon handed it back. I think Neva was startled that anyone would be so bold as to take a comb out of her hair.

It seemed like the old Pawnee in the black hat went on jabbering at Uncle Seth for an hour, though I suppose it was really only several minutes. Although Uncle Seth was perfectly polite I could see the vein working on the top of his nose.

"I think we better give them a plug of tobacco," he said—we had laid in several plugs when we passed through Omaha.

"Why?" Ma asked. "I wouldn't give *you* a plug, if you woke my baby."

"It's the custom, ma'am," Father Villy said.

"That's right—the custom," Uncle Seth said. "Throw in a little coffee too, Villy—but I think we better balk if they ask for bullets."

I guess the Pawnee did ask for bullets, because

the palaver went on for a good while, with the old headman doing the talking and the other Indians just prowling around, looking under the wagon and examining the mule harness. Finally Uncle Seth handed over the plug of tobacco, while Father Villy filled a little pouch with coffee beans.

"Go light on the coffee, Father," Ma said. "If I have to travel in a place with no trees without my coffee you'll all have to put up with a cranky woman—Seth knows how I get when I don't have my coffee."

"She's a regular Comanche when she's coffee starved," Uncle Seth said.

It was plain that the Pawnees had expected more in the way of presents than a plug of tobacco and a little pouch full of coffee beans, but that was all they got. The old headman grumbled, but once the warriors had fingered everything two or three times, they rode off toward the river, which was two or three miles south. Even after they slipped over the next ridge we could still hear the sleet crunching under their horses' hooves.

The plains were vast and white and gloomy, but at least the Indians were gone.

"Think how cold your head would be if they pulled your scalp off in weather like this," G.T. said, at which point Neva gave him the blackest look yet.

**6** I T was such a relief to us children to have the Indians gone that we all started yawning and could have gone right to sleep, had it not been that the adults took a different view of the matter.

"Now don't be yawning, boys—you've got to help Charlie guard the mules," Uncle Seth said. "I'll help Mary Margaret keep a lookout on the wagon, and Neva and Villy can just be general guards."

G.T. was much put out by that command.

"But the Indians left," he said. "You can hear them. They're heading for the river."

"Don't be presuming to instruct your elders, G.T.," Uncle Seth said. "Bothersome as the Pawnee is when you've got him in your camp, it's once he's left that you really have to worry. Go help Charlie with the mules."

"The clouds are coming back," Charlie said. "It won't be moonlight much longer—once it's dark they might try for a mule—I'm going to bring them in close to the wagon."

"I have never liked to sleep with a mule breathing on me," Ma said. "But I guess I can stand it if that's the best way to secure them."

The moon soon went behind a cloud, as Charlie had predicted; the only light was the faint white of the sleet and the flickers of our campfire. We hitched all six mules to the wagon, in a line—the two horses also. I stood between two mules, shivering, and G.T. did the same. Then I heard coyotes yipping. When I strained my eyes I thought I saw forms creeping around on the plain.

"Are those Pawnees?" I whispered to Charlie. I was sure we were about to be in a battle.

"No, those are coyotes," Charlie said.

Ma sat by the campfire, keeping the baby warm. She fed cow chips into the flames, one or two at a time.

It was during that night on the sleety prairies— it seemed to last for a week—that I really learned what cold was. All that saved me—and G.T. too— was the fact of being between the two mules. The cold just got colder and colder—the temperature dropped and dropped. It wasn't just my hands and feet that froze—it was my cheeks and eyelids, my forehead, my ears. It felt like the blood was freezing inside me. From time to time I stopped to rub my freezing cheeks against a warm mule.

G.T. had an even worse time than me. He forgot and grabbed his gun barrel with his bare hand: of course, he stuck to his gun and peeled a good strip of skin off two fingers when he tried to get loose. Ma rubbed a little antelope tallow on the skinned place. It was not until the first faint light came that Charlie told us we could go get warm.

The ends of Ma's hair had frozen where baby Marcy had breathed on it during the night.

"The Pawnees must have lost their starch," Uncle Seth observed. "Six fine mules and two horses and they didn't even manage to steal one. It's almost an insult."

"It was because of Villy," Charlie said. "They think he makes bad medicine."

"Yes, they have a powerful fear of the rosary," Father Villy said. "They associate it with funerals, mostly."

"Why, they stole my cowbell—I can't find it," Ma said.

"With that many Pawnees milling around, if all we lost is a cowbell we got off light," Uncle Seth said. "We don't have a cow anyway."

"No, but if we settle out here we might get a cow or two," Ma said. "It would be nice to have a cowbell, to help locate our cows with, if we get some."

That was the first any of us had heard about the prospect of settling out west. We had been on the move for a good while now, but none of us kids really knew what all this travel was leading to. Ma wanted to have a talk with Pa, we knew that—but what the talk was supposed to be about had us mystified. It was going to be an important talk, though—otherwise Ma would just have waited to have it next time Pa came home.

"It's for reasons of my own, Sherman," Ma said, the one time I got up the nerve to ask her about it. She wouldn't say more than that.

The band of Pawnees led by old Nose Turns Down never bothered us again, but it was not long before we began to see more Indians, lots of them, mainly traveling in small groups. Five or six would race up to us, feathers fluttering on their lances— feathers or sometimes scalps. All of them were bold when it came to inspecting our goods, a habit that continued to annoy Ma, who quarreled with Uncle Seth about it.

"Why wouldn't they ride right in?" he asked her. "There are no doors out here on the baldies—did you expect them to knock?"

"No, but I didn't expect them to be so familiar, either," Ma said.

"It's *their* country, Mary—we're the invaders, not them," Uncle Seth said, speaking more sharply than he usually spoke to Ma.

"I don't want their country—I just want to pass through," Ma said, a little surprised by his tone.

"We *are* passing through," Uncle Seth said. "Us and a lot more like us."

It was certainly true that plenty of people were headed in the same direction we were. Several times we even saw men walking: no more equipment than a rifle, a spade, and a blanket or two. There was a wagon train behind us, nearly as long as the one in front of us, and lots of single wagons like our own.

"I confess I'm shocked by the lack of game," Father Villy said. "It's only been five years since I traveled the Platte—only five years ago there was plenty of game."

"The same for me," Uncle Seth said. "When Dick and I first hauled freight to Fort Laramie we were never out of sight of critters we could eat. Buffalo, elk, antelope—when supper time came we just grabbed a rifle and shot whatever looked tastiest. Now about the only meat we can count on is prairie dogs."

Of course, we saw plenty of prairie dogs, but we hadn't killed one yet—Uncle Seth wouldn't let us shoot at them.

"I don't favor wasting bullets on small varmints," he said.

"The old days have always seemed better to people—I wonder why that is, Seth," Ma asked.

For once Uncle Seth seemed to have no opinion. He took his rifle and rode off to look for the game that he had just said wasn't there.

**7** W H I L E we were fixing our wagon for about the fourth time in a week, the thing that G.T. used to worry about finally happened: a bear sprang out and went for him. We had been struggling through what Father Villy called the malpais—he said it just meant "bad country," and this country was certainly bad, a land of dips and dry creeks and sharp rocky gullies. Some of the gullies were so hard to pull out of that we had to hitch all the mules to the wagon. The mules were up to this rough travel, but our old wagon wasn't. The dryness loosened the spokes, and they began to fall out of the wheels. Then one day, as we were easing up out of a steep gully, one of the rear wheels just suddenly came off and went rolling down the gully, in the direction of the Platte River.

When the wheel came off, the rear end of the wagon dropped and the wagon box shook loose and fell out, spilling most of my ma's cooking stuff. Marcy had been napping—before anyone could catch her she slid out of the back of the wagon and had the bad luck to land right on a little cactus.

"Whoa! Whoa! We're wrecked!" Uncle Seth said to Ma, who was driving. Ma stopped the mules, but I don't think she quite took in what had happened until she noticed the wagon wheel rolling off down the gully.

"Dern the luck, where does that wheel think it's going?" she said. "One of you boys go get it, quick."

Father Villy had just picked up the baby when the bear sprang out—it had been down in the gully, trying to dig out a ground squirrel, when the wagon wheel came rolling along and startled Mr. Bruin.

G.T. had just started to go retrieve the wheel when a brown bear that looked as big as a hill came roaring up toward him. What saved G.T. was Charlie Seven Days's little sorrel horse, which had the bad luck to be nibbling a little growth of bunchgrass on the side of the gully. Before the horse could move the bear whacked it like Ma might whack G.T. if her temper was up. The sorrel horse died on the spot, of a broken neck. G.T. was paralyzed: he couldn't move. It was his good luck that Uncle Seth happened to have his rifle in his hand, and that he was a skilled sharpshooter, too. You wouldn't think a little thing like a bullet could kill a bear that size, but Uncle Seth killed it with two shots. When the bear first sprang out it seemed to be right on us, but in fact it was a fair way down the gully. Uncle Seth's second shot caused it to sit down and look thoughtful. It pawed at itself for a moment and then flopped over, dead. Once killed, it didn't look half as big as it had looked while it was alive, but it was still twice as big as any bear you'd find in Missouri.

G.T. was so shocked he didn't realize he was alive. He couldn't even talk, for several minutes.

"This solves the vittles problem but not the wagon problem," Uncle Seth said. "If the wheel hadn't come off I doubt that bear would even have noticed us."

I guess Ma hadn't been as impressed by the bear as the rest of us were, besides which she was impatient by nature. Ma hated delays, even delays caused by grizzly bears.

"That bear's dead, G.T.—go on and get the wagon wheel," she said.

G.T. didn't even answer. I think he was still trying to convince himself he was alive.

"Leave him be, Mary Margaret," Uncle Seth said. "He's had a shock."

He and Charlie Seven Days eased down the gully and took a closer look at the bear. They had their guns at the ready, in case the bear was just playing possum.

"It's dead—I can see that much from here," Ma said. "What's everybody lolling around for? My wagon box is broken, my baby's full of cactus, that wagon wheel's probably still rolling, and you're all standing around looking at a dead bear. We need to get this wagon fixed or we'll still be in this gully tomorrow."

Neva, who was fearless if she was anything, finally went and got the wagon wheel, rolling it back up the gully it had just rolled down. If we hadn't had Father Villy, though, I doubt we could ever have got the wheel back on the wagon. He lifted the whole back end of the wagon and held it long enough for us to wedge the wheel back on.

The task of butchering the bear and the horse was left to Charlie, who was very quick and skillful with a skinning knife. He tried to show G.T. and I how to cut up a large animal—we were eager to try out our new knives—but we were so slow and did so many things wrong that Ma finally called off the lesson. Her lifelong habit of interfering with whatever happened to be going on irritated Uncle Seth sometimes, and this was one of the times.

"Don't you even want these boys to know how to cut up a bear?" he asked her.

"Not particularly," Ma said. "They might live the rest of their lives without needing to cut up another bear."

G.T. and I talked about that grizzly bear for the rest of our lives, but it was plain that it had made little impression on Ma.

"Good Lord, it was just a bear," she said. "It's no more inconvenient than having a baby fall on a cactus."

"It would have been if I hadn't been around to

shoot it," Uncle Seth pointed out. "At the very least it would have laid waste to the mules."

"Why make up notions about things that didn't happen?" Ma asked. "You *were* along to shoot it, and that's one reason you're along on this trip: so you can shoot things that need to be shot."

"I wish I was as practical as you are, Mary Margaret," Uncle Seth said. It was plain that Ma's bossy ways had put a strain on his temper, again.

"Well, you ain't, and that's that," Ma said, as if that settled the matter.

Not only was Charlie Seven Days the best at cutting up dead bears and dead horses, he also turned out to be the best at getting cactus thorns out of babies. He soaked them loose in some warm water and then rubbed some bear grease on Marcy's punctures, so she wouldn't be so whiny.

I guess knowing how to cure cactus punctures was what Ma considered a practical skill. She was real friendly to Charlie after that.

**8** A F T E R that morning when the bear sprang out it seemed like some little thing went wrong with the wagon every day. The rocks and the creeks and the gullies—the malpais, as Father Villy called it—were destroying our wagon a little at a time.

Ma knew it but she did her best to ignore it, waiting impatiently while Uncle Seth and Father Villy repaired the spoke or the hitch or the shaft—whatever went wrong on a given day.

"How far till we're done with this malpais?" she asked the priest. "I've had about enough of it."

"Another week, ma'am," Father Villy said.

Once again, though, it turned out that being a little distance back from a big wagon train was a piece of luck—our wagon wasn't the only conveyance to suffer. Almost every day us kids, while out with our turd sacks, would spot some little piece of equipment that had been dropped by the big train. Once we even found a whole wagon that had been abandoned. The Indians had picked it over some, but there were still lots of valuable parts that we could scavenge—and we did. Uncle Seth even broke up the bottom and sides, to use to patch the holes in our wagon bed.

"There's no reason for any part of the United States to be this big," Ma said one morning. A rear wheel had just come loose again, which meant a slow day.

"It's even bigger in some places," Father Villy said.

"I don't see how it could be bigger," Ma said, a position I agreed with. Sometimes we'd come to the top of a hill or ridge only to have the sky swell out above us and the horizon retreat so far away that it was hard to believe we could ever get across to it.

"Montana's bigger," Father Villy assured Ma.

"I hope my husband's had the good sense to stay out of Montana then," Ma said. Though the breakdowns vexed her, it was clear that she had no intention of giving up.

Of course, there would have been no advantage to giving up. We were so far out in the middle of nowhere that we would have been lucky to make it home, even if we turned back.

"How much farther to a house?" Ma asked, looking around her at the empty plain. "I've about forgotten what a house looks like."

It was a bright, clear day, but a chilly wind was howling out of the north.

"I guess you'd call Fort Laramie a house, of sorts," Uncle Seth said. "It's about a hundred miles away.

"I doubt you'll approve it, though," he added.

"Seth, nobody made you the judge of what I approve of," Ma said. "Or what I *don't* approve of, either."

"Maybe not, but I have spent several months of my life at Fort Laramie and it's a disorderly place, filled with cowards and drunkards and whores and coffee coolers, none of which you normally approve of," he said.

"Don't you talk of harlots around my boys," Ma said. "What's a coffee cooler?"

"It's an Indian who's too lazy to hunt," Uncle Seth said. "By now I imagine those Pawnees have cooled that coffee we gave them."

"Oh, you mean beggars," Ma said.

Just then Charlie Seven Days touched Uncle Seth's arm. Charlie had been afoot since the day the bear killed his horse, but he seemed just as happy to be walking. One day he killed a big porcupine—the meat tasted rank, but Charlie helped Neva pull out the quills, which he said could be used to ornament a shawl.

Charlie pointed to a ridge to the northwest—all I could see were some moving dots, but the dots soon turned out to be Indians, and they were moving our way fast. In fact they seemed to be charging right at us—Ma thought the same.

"Seth, they're charging," she said. "We better get ready to fight."

"It's the Bad Faces," Charlie said. "I see that paint horse that Red Cloud likes."

"You may be right," Father Villy said. He was as cool as if Charlie had just quoted a verse of scripture or something.

"Seth, did you hear me?" Ma asked. The fact that the horses were racing toward us at breakneck speed made more of an impression on Ma than the grizzly bear had.

"They're Sioux, Mary Margaret," Uncle Seth said. "They ain't attacking, they're just showing off their horsemanship. The Sioux ain't been cowed yet—they still think they have the right to run their horses, if they want to."

I wasn't as easy in my mind about the Indians as Uncle Seth was, but I had to admit it was a noble sight to see them come flashing over the prairies at reckless speed. I had never seen horses ridden so fast—when they came to a creek or small gully they soared over it like birds, the horses kicking up dust on the other side.

"I've heard the Comanches can outride the Sioux but I don't trust the report," Father Villy said. "Look at them come!"

For a moment I felt a lump in my throat, just from the beauty of the race—but I was scared, too. What if they all pulled tomahawks at the last minute and knocked us all dead? They were riding so low on their mounts that even if we had shot I doubt we'd have hit more than one or two of them, which wouldn't have been enough.

Then, when they were no more than fifteen or twenty wagon lengths from us, they stopped. A few of the horses were so caught up in the run that they pawed the air, anxious to keep going.

"Red Cloud is behind," Charlie said. "So is Old Man Afraid."

We saw that two of the Sioux riders hadn't been quite so swift. They were a half mile back, coming at a slow, easy lope.

"These here's just the youngsters," Uncle Seth said. "They *will* race their nags."

"Who's going to palaver?" Father Villy asked.

We all looked at Charlie, but he declined the position. He just stood close to the wagon, watching the Sioux.

Then the two older men eased to the front of the crowd, waiting for someone from our bunch to go talk to them.

"Seth, go on—talk to them," Ma said.

The two older Indians who were waiting to talk to us didn't seem impatient. The one on the paint horse had a narrow face and carried a brand-new rifle—a repeater of some kind. The other Indian was older—his face was wrinkled, like a melon gets when the sun has dried it up.

Uncle Seth and Father Villy walked out together and began to sign to the Indians. The signing went on for a while, and then the thin-faced man on the paint horse began to talk—and did he talk! He sat right there on his horse and made a long speech—I didn't get a word of it, and I doubt anyone else did, either, unless it was Father Villy.

The speech went on for so long that I expected Ma to get impatient—she didn't enjoy listening to anyone for much of a length of time—but for once she behaved herself and waited for the discussion to be over.

The minute it *was* over the young Sioux warriors came crowding around the wagon, just as the Pawnees had done. Uncle Seth gave them a lot of tobacco and plenty of coffee too—Ma didn't complain. Uncle Seth even gave the two leaders hunting knives, like the ones G.T. and I had.

"Why do they call them Bad Faces?" Neva wanted to know, when the Sioux left. They were in sight for a long time, riding north.

"I'd like to know that too," Ma said. "They were the best-looking Indians I've seen—except for Charlie."

I expect she just said that to be polite, since Charlie just looked like an ordinary man.

"It's just a name for Red Cloud's bunch," Father Villy said.

"That doesn't explain a thing," Ma said.

In fact, though Uncle Seth and Father Villy had made a show of being cordial, neither of them looked very happy once the Sioux had gone.

"I hope Dick Cecil's at Fort Laramie," Uncle Seth said. "That would be the lucky thing."

"Why?" Ma asked.

"It's those forts the army's putting up along the Bozeman Trail," Father Villy said. "It's foolish—foolish."

"If it's so foolish why are they putting them up?" Ma asked.

"If you knew anything about the army, Mary Margaret, you'd know that they do foolish things every day," Uncle Seth said. "I doubt myself that the army ever does anything that *isn't* foolish—and

I was a soldier in that same army for four years."

"There's another point," Father Villy said, "which is that the farther west they go, the less brains the army uses. There's been a gold strike in Montana, which means miners will be hurrying up the Bozeman Trail—only it ain't their trail! You've heard of the Holy Land, I expect, haven't you, ma'am?"

"*I* have," Neva said. "It's where Cain slew Abel."

"Well, we think of it for other things besides murder," Father Villy said. "But you're right—it's where Cain slew Abel."

"I don't see the application," Ma said.

"It's that the army's built these new forts in the Sioux Holy Land," Father Villy said. "That's what Red Cloud was telling us in that long speech he made. What he said was that the Sioux won't stand for it—or the Cheyenne either."

"They're going to go for the new forts—ain't that what you think, Charlie?" Uncle Seth said.

Charlie Seven Days just nodded.

"A white man in a fever to get to the diggings will always try to go by the quickest way, even when the quickest way means going right through the Sioux," Uncle Seth said.

"Yes, even if quick travel means his scalp," Father Villy said.

"I guess I finally understand you," Ma said. "If Dick happens to be hauling to one of these new forts, then he's in plenty of danger—is that correct?"

"*Plenty* of danger, ma'am," Father Villy said.

**9** A F T E R our meeting with the Bad Faces, Ma let all of us know that she was not going to tolerate any lollygagging or needless delays in our trip to find Pa. The Bad Faces had impressed her, but they didn't fool her. They could have killed us easy—it was just our luck that all Red Cloud wanted to do was make a speech.

It was Ma's frustration that the country we were moving through just wasn't made for hurry. The harder we tried to pour on the speed, the more the country seemed to work against us. One night four of our mules slipped their hobbles—it took Charlie half a day to track them and bring them back.

Then it rained for three straight days. All the way we had hugged the Platte River, to be sure of water, but lack of water ceased to be our problem: too much water was our problem. Every little trickle of a creek became a river; ground that had been hard as flint became mud. If we had not had four strong mules we would never have got the wagon out of some of the mud holes it sank into. At least there were trees here and there again, so we could enjoy a good wood fire at night.

When we first saw the mountains way up ahead, after such a stretch of time on the plains, we didn't really know what we were seeing. The minute the first mountains appeared G.T. wanted to run on and climb one—he had to be persuaded that they were still forty miles away.

Ma was often vexed by the rain and the mud, but she never wavered; she drove the wagon all day, refusing to let anyone spell her—at least, she did until we finally came to Laramie Fork—with the fort at last in sight—and faced a regular flood of water, moving too fast for even a strong mule team to try and struggle through.

"Damn the luck," Uncle Seth said. "We could all sleep warm and dry in Fort Laramie tonight if this little creek wasn't up.

"Most of the time a man can jump this creek— but now look!" he added.

"I see a washtub," G.T. said, pointing into the froth of the water. "Here comes the washboard, too."

"Well, grab it, somebody," Ma said. "We can always use an extra washtub."

The fact was, the little river seemed to be floating lots of goods right past us.

"It's a regular store," Ma said. "Grab that rolling pin."

"That wagon train probably tried to cross upstream," Father Villy said. "Somebody's wagon turned over."

At Ma's urging, me and G.T. partly stripped off and got in the water, which was so cold it turned us numb in a minute. I did manage to grab the wash-tub, though, and G.T. caught the washboard. Charlie reached in and snagged a pitchfork without even getting wet. When G.T. and I finally got out of the water our teeth were chattering like bones.

"So what do we do now, Seth?" Ma asked.

"We do the thing you hate most: wait," Uncle Seth said. "We'll wait for the water to go down."

"When do you expect it to fall?" Ma asked.

"I can't predict," he said. "Maybe this afternoon, maybe tomorrow. What do you think, Charlie?"

"Tomorrow," Charlie said. "Unless it rains more."

"I can't wait that long," Ma said. "We've been traveling all this time to get to Fort Laramie, and there it is. This is not deep water. I believe I can get through it if I push hard."

We could all see that Uncle Seth was nearly to the point of losing his temper with Ma. The big vein on his nose was wiggling like a worm.

"It ain't how deep it is, it's how fast it's flowing, Mary Margaret," he said. "It might push this wagon right over, and then you and the baby and everything else we own will just float away."

It was clear that Ma didn't believe him. She still had the reins in her hand, and it seemed that any minute she might defy his advice and take the plunge.

Uncle Seth was so vexed by her stubbornness

that it looked for a minute like he meant to jump up on the wagon seat and grab the reins from her before she could pop the mules. Ma had something in her—something terrible—that just wouldn't be stopped—not by Pa or Uncle Seth or argument or a raging river or anything else; but this time, before it came to a crisis between the two of them, there was a commotion upstream.

"Look, Arapaho," Father Villy said.

While we had been dragging washtubs out of the creek what seemed like a whole Indian village had arrived upstream. It was the howling of all their dogs that we finally heard, over the sound of the water. The roaring creek that had stopped us made no impression on the Arapaho: the water was just boiling with them. The women had long poles attached to their horses, with baskets of some kind hung between them.

"I want to see this," Ma said, turning the wagon.

We all went up to watch—a stretch of the river was just full of dogs and horses and Indians. Some of the dogs even had skinny little poles attached to them, with smaller baskets between *their* poles. The large baskets, the ones the horses were pulling, had babies in them, and puppies, and here and there an old man or an old woman, sitting as high in the baskets and bundles as they could get, but not high enough to keep them out of the water. Soon babies were screeching and spluttering at the shock of the icy water. Puppies were whining, dogs howling, horses whinnying; but the Indian women were mainly quiet. Once I saw a baby pop out of its basket but its mother just reached back and plucked it out of the water. She settled it back in its basket as if it had been a puppy.

The dogs were having the hardest time making the crossing, especially those with the drag poles attached to them. The current carried some of the dogs down abreast of us, but the dogs kept struggling and all of them finally reached shore.

"It's only women—where are the men?" Ma asked.

"Oh, the men are most likely already at Fort Laramie, loafing," Uncle Seth said. "If not, they might be hunting, or making a little war, somewhere. They wouldn't concern themselves with a little thing like getting their wives and babies through a flood."

So far as I could tell the Indians didn't lose a baby, or an old person, or even a dog, in crossing the raging stream. This fact was not lost on Ma.

"Well, if *their* menfolk ain't concerned I don't guess you need to be either, Seth," Ma said, and she immediately put our wagon in the water right behind the last of the Indian women. Just before she hit the river Uncle Seth jumped on Sally and grabbed Marcy out of the wagon—he didn't want to risk having her pop out like the Indian baby had.

"Let's go, boys—there's no stopping her!" he said.

Ma had hitched two mules to the wagon, which left G.T. and I each a mule. Neva was up on the wagon seat, beside Ma—Father Villy and Charlie Seven Days just had to wade it. Ma had crossed quite a few creeks by this time, and knew how to urge on the mules. Soon she was in midstream and doing fine. The only trouble came when one of the last of the Indian dogs took a dislike to Little Nicky and came swimming back to snarl and nip at him. Little Nicky didn't appreciate this attention—he tried to paw the dog, which, for a moment, threatened to tip the wagon. Uncle Seth was too far back to help. What saved the situation was an Indian woman, who saw Ma's predicament and turned back to help her. She grabbed the snarly dog by its scruff and pulled him off. It looked for a minute or two that the mules might balk anyway, but Ma yelled at them and popped them hard with the reins, which convinced them that the better move would be to get out of the chilly water. The helpful Arapaho woman stayed right in front of them and guided them across. The dog soon escaped her, but he didn't bother Nicky again—he had enough to do just getting on across the creek.

Ma's only real trouble came when she had already reached the other bank—the right rear wheel seemed to drop into a hole between two rocks, just at the edge of the stream. We all ended up having to wade in and lift and push—it was as if that wheel had taken root in its hole. We had to hitch up the other two mules before that wheel popped free.

"It's a lucky thing those nice Indians came along," Ma said to Uncle Seth. "Otherwise, you and me would still be arguing."

"No, otherwise you would have drowned yourself, the baby, and most of the mules," he said.

**10** I THOUGHT forts were for soldiers—all I see is Indians," Ma said, when we were a hundred yards or so from the gates of Fort Laramie.

"The soldiers are inside, drunk," Uncle Seth said. "The Indians are outside, drunk. It might be different in Missouri, but that's how forts work in Wyoming."

Once we finally got out of the creek and were trying to get dry, it started to snow. By the time we got on dry clothes and started on for the fort it was nearly dusk. Several bunches of Indians were camped outside the fort, on the plain in front of it. The smoke from many campfires rose as the snow fell, so that the lower sky all seemed to melt together, smoke and snow and dusk, making it hard to get a clear look at anything. Indian dogs were everywhere, nipping and snarling at one another. Two or three of the campfires belonged to trappers, with hide wagons sitting beside them—a few of the trappers were as hairy as Father Villy. Some nodded over their campfires—a few threw dice on a deerskin.

I had never expected to see such a wild sight in my life—neither had Neva, or G.T. I kept a good hold on my mule—I didn't want the nipping dogs to spook him. When we were nearly to the gates we passed the very Arapahos who had led us across the stream—most of them already had their lodges up. We even saw the very mongrel who had tried to bite Nicky—he was quarreling with another dog over a scrap of hide. The woman who pulled him off Nicky and then led us across had just whacked a fat puppy in the head and was getting it ready for the pot.

"IIey!" Neva said, outraged at the thought that someone would eat a pup. She had tried to rear several puppies, only to lose them to the coyotes—there were so many varmints around Boone's Lick that pets didn't have much of a chance. We all knew that Indians ate dogs, but this was the first chance we had to witness how short life could be for a puppy in an Indian camp.

"Have *you* eaten puppies?" Neva asked Father Villy—she had come to regard him as her special friend.

"Yes, miss—they're tender," the priest said.

Before Neva could question him further we passed through the big gates into the broad quadrangle of the fort; suddenly we were *inside* some place, for the first time in weeks. It was a large stockade, with room for hundreds of men and plenty of animals, but we had had nothing but the broad plains around us for weeks on end. Being inside the fort felt a little close.

A burly soldier carrying a carbine came walking over to challenge us—he wobbled a little, when he walked. Ma pulled up and waited.

"Hello, Ned—have you come to arrest us?" Uncle Seth asked.

Hearing his name called out seemed to startle the big soldier. Then he noticed Ma on the wagon seat—it was snowing heavily enough that he had missed that detail—and he quickly stopped and took his cap off. He opened his mouth to speak but only came out with a big rumbling belch.

"Seth, is that you? It's dim light," the soldier said. He had a glassy-eyed look. When he tipped his cap to Ma he lost control of it—the cap floated down into the mud, which seemed to embarrass the man greatly.

"Pardon me, ma'am," he said. "I believe I've gone and et too much."

When he reached down to pick up his cap he fell flat on his face in the mud—he didn't move. Ma had to turn the mules just to get around him.

"Dead drunk, I fear," Father Villy said. "It's a frequent failing of our soldiers in these lonely outposts."

"Lonely—I wouldn't say it's lonely," Ma remarked. "There's more people camped around here than live in Boone's Lick, Missouri, I'd say."

She was right about that. As many folks were camped inside the fort as outside—soldiers, trappers, a few people with wagons, Indian women, dogs. Some sturdy cabins lined two sides of the big stockade, but most of the people seemed to be living outdoors.

"Who runs this fort, Seth?" Ma asked. "I want to find him quick and inquire about my husband."

"General Slade runs it—Sam Slade," Uncle Seth said. "At least, he did the last time I was here—I suppose he might have been replaced. But I don't know that we can just barge in and get an audience with General Slade, if he's here—we don't need to anyway," he said. "Any of these fellows who's sober enough to stand up will know if Dick's around."

"Then find someone sober and ask them," Ma said. "And if there's a room empty anywhere, ask them if we can use it for the night. I'm tired of sleeping with snow in my hair."

"Why, here's Johnny Molesworth—I expect he can help us," Father Villy said. "I see he's been made a captain."

A slim soldier stepped out of the gloom of smoke and snow and evening light and grabbed Father Villy by the hand.

"Villy, what a pleasure," he said. "I see your beard's matured."

Then the young captain noticed Ma and Neva, took off his cap, and made them a little bow.

"Hello, ladies—welcome to our muddy old fort," he said. "I'm surprised you got across Laramie Fork—we've had a regular stream of people who nearly drowned out."

"Some Indians helped us," Ma said. "I'm Mary Margaret Cecil—I guess you know Seth."

"He should know me—he put me in jail the last

time we met," Uncle Seth said, in a chilly tone.

Captain Molesworth ignored the chilly tone and grabbed Uncle Seth's hand.

"Now, Seth, it was just for your own protection," the captain said. "I was afraid one of those thieving Canadian skunks might shoot you."

"Forgiven. Where's Dick?" Uncle Seth asked. "Mary Margaret is his wife and she's come a far piece to talk to him. We expected to find him here."

Captain Molesworth seemed a little startled by that information—he looked at Ma in surprise.

"No, Dick's not here," he said. "He's wood hauling up at Fort Phil Kearny—it's one of our fine new forts, just finished," he said. "Dick went up with Colonel Carrington—they're predicting a hard winter and Colonel Carrington was eager to lay in lots of wood."

"Drat the man—how far is that?" Ma asked.

"Oh, it isn't far—the distance wouldn't be the problem," the captain said.

Ma just looked at him and waited.

"The Sioux would be the problem," he went on. "They're testy with us over these forts."

"That's right," Father Villy said. "We ran into Red Cloud and he told us as much himself."

"The Cheyenne are fractious too—it's a dilemma," the young soldier said.

"For you, maybe—not for me," Ma said. "I didn't build the forts. Is there a room we can bunk in for the night? I expect we'll press on tomorrow."

"We do have a cabin, recently vacated," the captain said. "Let me get someone to see to your livestock—we're lucky to have plenty of good fodder."

"Now listen, Mary Margaret," Uncle Seth began, as soon as Captain Molesworth walked off to find someone to tend our stock.

"Listen to what?" Ma asked. "You better not try to talk me out of going to wherever Dick is—that's the one reason I've dragged everybody all this way."

"That wasn't my point, that's another point," Uncle Seth said. "This wagon has been about shook to pieces—we need to give it over to the care of a skilled blacksmith for a day or two, or one of these days the whole bottom will drop out and we'll all be in a pickle."

"I wouldn't mind resting for a day, but no longer," Ma said. "If you do locate a blacksmith, instruct him to hurry—a day's all I can allow him."

Captain Molesworth was soon back with two soldiers who took charge of our mules. Then he showed us where we would be staying—a big cabin with a loft just like ours at home. There was a good fireplace, but no fire in it yet.

"Why, this is a palace—I'm surprised it's vacant with so many people milling around in these parts," Ma said.

"Just vacant two days—a sad case—suicide," the young officer said. "I guess some people find the winter glooms too hard to bear, around here."

"It was a woman, wasn't it?" Ma asked, looking around the room.

"Why yes—a young woman, married less than a year," Captain Molesworth said. "How could you tell?"

"It's just a feeling I had," Ma said.

**11** T W O  soldiers wheeled over a little cart stacked with firewood and we soon had a roaring fire going in our cabin. Nobody could find Charlie Seven Days—he had dropped off to visit with some of the Indians outside the fort—but Uncle Seth and Father Villy went off to pay their respects to General Slade. Captain Molesworth invited us all to partake of the officers' mess, but Neva was the only one who went—Ma even found a ribbon to tie in her hair.

I was hungry and would have liked to eat with the officers but once we were in our cabin, with the good fire going, a tiredness came over me like none I had ever felt before. I wanted food, but the thought of walking even two hundred yards to the mess hall seemed too much. I believe G.T. felt the same. Ma handed me a little piece of bear meat jerky, but when I put it in my mouth I found I was too tired to chew. Ma later claimed she had to yank the jerky out of my mouth to keep me from choking, and it was probably true. After so many weeks in the open, the warmth of the room put me right to sleep.

When I woke the next morning bright sunlight was streaming in the windows of the cabin. Neva had come home at some point—she was dead to the world, with her feet nearly in the fire. I didn't see Ma or G.T.—they were both early risers. The snow had stopped. When I looked out the windows I saw blue sky. The air outside was chilly.

I supposed Ma and G.T. had probably walked off to the blacksmith's; no doubt Ma wanted to give the man a few instructions and make sure he meant to have the work finished by the end of the day.

It took my eyes a moment to adjust to the sharp sunlight. I thought I'd just explore the fort and maybe get a better look at some of the Indians camped around it. With the snow falling and all the smoke blowing around I hadn't been able to see them well. It occurred to me that if I could locate the mess hall they might give me coffee and a biscuit—maybe even a little bacon.

I had hardly gone ten steps when I spotted Ma, way up by the north wall of the stockade. She seemed to be talking to a plump young Indian woman who had a lodge of skins built against the poles of the blockade. A girl a little younger than

Neva had a skin of some kind pegged out and was scraping it with a knife. The snow had mostly melted, but two little girls were toddling around in what was left of it—one of them was Marcy, who had long since got her walking legs under her and could be counted on to wander off just when it was most inconvenient to retrieve her.

Ma motioned for me to come over. While I was walking across the wide quadrangle Ma squatted down on her haunches—she was watching the little Indian girl, who was just Marcy's height. The young Indian woman seemed to be enjoying the sight of two toddlers, playing in the melting snow.

"Come look at this fine little girl—she's Sioux," Ma said, still squatting.

The child was a pert little creature, with bright black eyes. She and Marcy would stare at one another, solemn as judges, and then go dashing off to the nearest patch of snow.

"What do you think, Shay?" Ma asked.

Ma didn't seem angry, as she watched the little girls. She just seemed kind of bemused.

"They're just the right age to be playmates," I said.

"I think they're a little more than playmates," Ma said. "Take a closer look."

It wasn't easy to get a closer look, because the two little girls were rushing around, squealing and kicking up snow whenever they came to it, but when I got them stopped and looked at them close I saw what Ma was getting at. Except for the fact that the little Indian girl was copper colored and

Marcy white, they *did* look like more than play-mates. They looked like twins. What startled me most, once I stooped down to look, was that both girls had a deep dimple in their chins—the same as I had, and G.T., and Neva, and Pa.

"That's Dick's dimple," Ma said. "These little girls are half sisters, like me and Rosie. This is your father's other family—or one of them—that we've come so far to meet."

It must have been true, because the young girl who was scraping the hide was using one of Pa's old knives.

"Oh, you oaf!" Neva said, when I woke her and told her the news.

# BOOK III
# The Holy Hills

**1** T H A T night it came another snow, a snow so thick and deep that it muffled the sounds of the fort. Even Ma, still eager to get north, saw there was no point in pushing off into it, though Father Villy and Charlie Seven Days did just that. Seeing them leave was almost as hard as watching Aunt Rosie sail on up the Missouri River at Omaha. I guess we all hoped they would travel on with us to Fort Phil Kearny, but that wasn't the direction they wanted to go. Charlie Seven Days had to report to the Old Woman, whose son he couldn't locate, and Father Villy still had it in his head to visit Siberia, which wasn't in the direction we were going.

"We're grateful for your help in getting this far," Ma said.

Neva cried the most, when they left. She had enjoyed having Father Villy teach her those French songs.

"Don't stay long in the north," Charlie said. He spoke a little sternly. "There will be trouble in the north."

"I second that opinion. Good-bye," Father Villy said.

With just a wave, they were gone.

"People *will* come and go," Uncle Seth said. I think he was just trying to get Ma to ease up on him a little. It turned out that Uncle Seth had known about Pa's Indian family all along, but had never mentioned it, a fact that put Ma in a stiff mood with him, for a day or two.

She was also annoyed with the blacksmith, an independent Yankee who refused to be hurried when it came to repairing our wagon.

"I'll fix what I can fix when I can fix it," he said, and that was all he said.

Neva and G.T. and I were glad enough not to have to rush right off from the fort. We liked watching the soldiers drill, and the Indians and trappers mill around. But the best part of our stay was getting to know Pa's Indian family, which was just about a perfect match for his Missouri family—that is, us. Marcy got to play with her little toddling half sister, Meadow Mouse, and Neva learned to scrape hides with her half sister Lark Sings, and Ma visited with Pa's Sioux wife, who was called Stones-in-the-Water. There was no language they both could talk in, but they seemed to enjoy just observing one another's children and looking at one another's things.

It was not until the evening of the day of the big snow that G.T. and I discovered that we even had half brothers, nearly our own age—one was named Blue Crow and the other He Sleeps. It was Uncle Seth who explained the Sioux names to us. The two boys wanted to take us right out hunting, which Ma allowed, although I believe she was nervous about it. Of course, He Sleeps and Blue Crow had fast horses and rode them at top speed, like those Bad Faces had ridden that day when Red Cloud made his long speech.

G.T. and I only had our mules for mounts—we couldn't really keep up, but the hunt turned out to be lucky anyway, and the wildest fun. He Sleeps spotted a big elk calf that had floundered into a deep snowdrift and worn itself out trying to escape. The calf was soon dispatched with hatchets, a bloody sight. Although G.T. and I hadn't really killed the big calf we were allowed to take a share back to Ma.

The fact that we all liked Pa's Indian family didn't make it any less a sore spot with Ma that Uncle Seth had never told her about it, even though He Sleeps was as old as me and Uncle Seth had known about Stones-in-the-Water all along.

"I'm a rattler but not a tattler," Uncle Seth said, in his own defense. "It is not my place to go blabbing about something that's none of my business."

"I guess that means you think it's right for a man to have two wives—is that so, Seth?" Ma asked.

"Well, it's the custom out here in the baldies," Uncle Seth said.

"Oh, I see," Ma said—I was listening from the loft. "The custom—like handing out tobacco and coffee when some Indians come for a visit. I suppose you think handing out a woman is no different from handing out coffee."

"In patriarch times a man was allowed several wives, I believe," Uncle Seth said calmly. "It's in the Bible."

"What if I don't want to go by the Bible?" Ma asked.

This shook G.T., who was proud of the fact that he had been baptized in the Missouri River.

"Everybody's supposed to go by the Bible," he yelled down. He was in the loft too. Neva was down by the fire, sitting with her new sister Lark Sings. They were playing with the porcupine quills.

"I don't need your opinion, G.T.," Ma said. "Who told you to preach to your mother?"

"You'll go to hell for sure, if you don't go by the Bible," G.T. yelled. He had once heard a fiery preacher and had been worried about hellfire ever since.

"What I want to know is, is this the limit of it, or has he got another family up there where he's hauling wood?" Ma asked.

"I've never been to Fort Phil Kearny, it was just built," Uncle Seth said. "How would I know?"

"You said the same thing in Omaha—but you *did* know!" Ma reminded him.

"I don't think Dick's partial to sleeping alone in

chilly weather," Uncle Seth said, cautiously. He was nursing a bottle of whiskey that he had procured somewhere. While I was watching, Ma reached over and took his bottle—it surprised him. She took a big swig and spat it into the fireplace, which caused the flames to leap up. Then she took another long swig, and this one she didn't spit out.

"Do you love me, Seth?" Ma asked. "That's my final question."

The question gave us all a start—Uncle Seth most of all.

"Mary, all these young ones are listening," he said.

"Let 'em! My children are old enough to know the facts of life," Ma said. "All except Marcy, and she's asleep. Are you going to answer?"

"Yes," he said.

"Yes, you're going to answer—or yes, you love me?" Ma asked.

"Both," Uncle Seth replied.

"All right—it's not bold but I guess it's an answer," Ma said.

"Mary Margaret, I'm too nervous to speak of such things in front of the children," Uncle Seth said.

It was easy to see that he was in a strain.

Ma took another long swallow and handed him back the bottle.

"We all have to live for ourselves—I want my children to hear that," Ma said. "As for you, have another drink. If you get a little drunker, maybe you'll feel a little bolder."

"Well, Dick *is* my brother," Uncle Seth said.

"I don't care what he is," Ma said. "We've lived this lie too long. I want it to end and I want it to end now!"

Whether it ended or not I don't know—I'm not even sure what the lie was. All I know is that the next morning Uncle Seth was out early, trying to get that independent Yankee blacksmith to hurry up with our wagon, so we could leave for the north.

**2** T H E  big soft snow had nearly melted
by the time we got our wagon back and
got it loaded. Nearly every officer in the
fort, including General Slade, came by to try and
talk Ma out of traveling north—they made the
journey seem like sure death for all of us—but they
might as well have been talking to a stump.

"Madam, there's no call for this intrepidity,"
General Slade said. "You might at least wait for
Colonel Fetterman—he's going that way soon to
reinforce Colonel Carrington. He'll be happy to escort you safely in."

"No, he wouldn't be happy to escort me anywhere," Ma said. "He'd be happier if he could just
knock me in the head."

General Slade didn't know that Ma and Colonel

Fetterman had had a sharp exchange in the black-smith's shop the day before. Ma was harrying the blacksmith to finish up with our wagon when Colonel Fetterman rode in and demanded that his horse be shod immediately.

"Just let me finish this little bit of work on the lady's wagon," the blacksmith said. Ma had been riding him all day—he was anxious to get rid of her, even if it meant sending her off to get scalped.

"Damn the work and damn the lady," Colonel Fetterman said. "I cannot fight wild savages on a lame horse, and this horse has been limping all morning due to improper shoes."

Colonel Fetterman didn't know that Ma was there—she was behind the forge, standing in the shadow, and I was with her.

The blacksmith tried to signal the colonel but the warning came too late.

"You can damn me till you're hoarse, Colonel, but I was here first and I mean to insist on service," Ma said.

Uncle Seth was some distance away, chatting with Captain Molesworth, but I guess he knew trouble was developing because he turned and came over to the blacksmith's shop.

Colonel Fetterman's face turned dark when he saw Ma, but he didn't withdraw his remark, or apologize for it either.

"You've no business interfering with the needs of the army, and I'll have no impertinent comments," he said. "This is a military fort and if I was in command of it I'd have every last one of you damn settlers driven out of it. You belong outside the walls, with the trappers and the other riffraff."

He turned and glared at Uncle Seth, who stopped and stood his ground, but didn't speak.

I guess the blacksmith felt like he was between a rock and a hard place because he began to hammer as hard as he could on the rim he was fitting on one of our wagon wheels. He must have decided that his welfare depended on finishing our wagon in the next minute or two—any longer delay and either Ma or Colonel Fetterman would be sure to ride him hard.

The big corporal named Ned, who had fallen down drunk the day we arrived, happened to be standing nearby, trying to comb some burrs out of his horse's tail.

"Damn you, if you won't work I'll have you jailed!" Colonel Fetterman said, to the blacksmith. "Get over here, Corporal, and take this man to jail. Then find someone competent to shoe my horse."

At this point Uncle Seth decided it might be well to try and change the subject.

"Say, Colonel Fetterman, young John Molesworth here has been telling me what a hand you are to fight Indians."

Maybe Uncle Seth thought a little flattery would improve the man's mood—but it didn't.

"Mind your own business, sir," Colonel Fetterman said. "I have a matter of military discipline to attend to here—and it's urgent."

Uncle Seth winked at Ma—the colonel didn't see it.

"All right, but I'm anxious to know your opinion of the Sioux as cavalrymen," Uncle Seth said. "There's some out here in the windies who rate them high. I've even heard one military man say that they're the best light cavalry in the world—is that your opinion?"

The comment at least got the colonel's attention.

"Whoever said that was a goddamn fool," Colonel Fetterman said. "A bunch of naked savages on horseback don't amount to a cavalry. I could take eighty men and whip the whole Sioux nation—and I hope I get the chance."

"And I hope you don't!" Ma said. It was plain the rude colonel had raised her temper pretty high.

Colonel Fetterman's face turned nearly purple—the fact that a woman would speak to him that way left him too annoyed to talk.

"Mary . . ." Uncle Seth said. I believe he meant to caution her about speaking so sharply to Colonel Fetterman, but his warning came too late. The fat was in the fire.

"Corporal, arrest this damn woman too, while you're at it," Colonel Fetterman said—he was practically spluttering, he was so angry.

Ned, the big corporal, was still holding the curry comb he had been using to rake burrs out of his horse's tail. I'm not sure he even realized he was supposed to arrest the blacksmith, but he did realize that it would be irregular if he had to arrest Ma.

"What for, Colonel?" he asked.

"For the use of treasonous language," Colonel

Fetterman said. I guess it was all he could come up with on the spur of the moment.

Ma walked right up to him—for a moment I thought she might slap the colonel, but all she did was stare him down.

"If a rude swaggerer like you was ever given the command of eighty men I have no doubt you'd promptly get them killed," she said.

Then she motioned for the blacksmith to get on with his work and walked away, grabbing Uncle Seth by the arm as she went.

Colonel Fetterman just stood there, black with rage. Ned, the big corporal, didn't move a muscle.

Three days later, when we were slogging up the muddy plain, Colonel Fetterman and his relief troop passed us. There looked to be about eighty men in the command.

"There goes that fellow who wanted to get you arrested for treason," Uncle Seth said.

"Yes—I have no doubt he would have had me shot, if it had been his say," Ma said.

She had changed her attitude and was letting Uncle Seth drive the mules.

I guess all the soldiers knew Colonel Fetterman was mad at Ma, because the troop passed us at a gallop and not a single soldier waved or looked our way.

**3** OUR first night out from Fort Laramie we got a big surprise—just at dusk, as we were building our campfire, we heard horses coming and our two half brothers, Blue Crow and He Sleeps, came racing into camp. He Sleeps had snuck up on a fat goose, on some little skim of a prairie pond, and they brought it to us as a going-away present.

We were all glad to see them, even Ma. The goose was mighty tasty, and the boys spent the evening trying to improve our command of sign language— or at least, Neva's command. She had already learned it and could make her fingers fly when talking to Blue Crow, the more talkative of our half brothers. G.T., though, had no skill with his hands—Blue Crow laughed until he cried at G.T.'s attempts to use a few simple signs. He Sleeps was the more solemn of the two—he was in awe of Ma and behaved very politely in her company.

"I don't need to learn sign language, I'm a Baptist anyway," G.T. said, when we got tickled at his crude efforts.

"Maybe so, but where you're going the Baptists have kind of thinned out," Uncle Seth said.

Despite the chill, we were all glad to be out of the fort. Some of the soldiers were civil, but some weren't. He Sleeps caught a tiny little field mouse and taught us a game involving three cups. The field mouse was under one of them: the point of the game was to guess which cup hid the mouse. He Sleeps moved the cups so fast the confused little mouse didn't have time to run. Neva beat both He Sleeps and Blue Crow, which didn't please them, particularly. When G.T. tried it he got so annoyed at guessing wrong that he finally knocked over the cups and let the mouse get away.

Ma didn't play—she liked watching the two Indian boys.

"That boy's got more than Dick's dimple, he's got his mischief, too," she said, referring to Blue Crow.

He Sleeps and Blue Crow rode with us for most of a fine bright morning—we were soon in higher country, though the big mountains were still just shadows in the far distance. Then the two boys turned their horses and went racing back toward Fort Laramie. Neva liked both of them—I believe she enjoyed having two new brothers to pester. She signed for a while, trying to get them to come north with us, but they just shook their heads. He Sleeps even made us a little speech—it may have been a warning.

"I believe he's of the same opinion as Red Cloud," Uncle Seth commented. "The one thing folks agree about is that there's going to be trouble at them new forts."

"There sure is, and I'm going to make some of it myself, once I find Dick," Ma said.

That afternoon we started an antelope and G.T. shot it—it was the biggest thrill of his life, up to that time.

"It was just that critter's bad luck that he ran into a Baptist," Uncle Seth said.

One thing Neva and G.T. and I talked about a lot, when we were off to ourselves, was Pa's other family. We wanted to know the same thing Ma wanted to know: if he had one extra family, what if he had more? Maybe he had two or three.

"Or eight," G.T. said.

"Not eight, you oaf!" Neva said. "Nobody could have eight families. There wouldn't be time."

"I wish there *was* eight and I wish you belonged to another one, not this one," G.T. said. He had about all he could take of Neva.

"I believe I'll start one with Bill Hickok when we get back," Neva said. She never tired of reminding us that Mr. Hickok had bought her two beefsteaks in one night.

I didn't think Pa had eight families, but I did ponder the whole business, as we made our way north, toward the high mountains. Sometimes I got to feeling real uneasy, at the thought of what Ma might be planning, once she found Pa. I knew she wouldn't have traveled so far, through all the dangers, if she didn't have something serious on her mind. But the only person I could have asked about it, other than Ma herself, was Uncle Seth, and he wasn't as available for questions as he had been in the past.

For one thing, since Ma had decided she was ready to let him drive the team, he seldom left Ma's side. The two of them sat there on the wagon seat all day, as we plodded along, leaving the rest of us to look after ourselves—Marcy included. She was weaned now, so Ma didn't have to pay such close attention to her. Marcy could also walk, which meant that she spent most of her time wandering off into trouble. She irritated the mules so much, pulling their tails and stomping around under their bellies, that it was a full-time job for one person, trying to keep her from getting kicked or bitten.

When it came to Ma and Pa and their differences, Neva held the most extreme opinion: she thought Ma meant to shoot Pa.

"That's what I would do if I was her and found out he had another wife—maybe two other wives," Neva said. "I wouldn't have it for a minute, not me!"

"Sassafras," I said. "You saw Ma with Stones-in-the-Water. The two of them got along fine."

"I'll stick to my opinion," Neva said.

I didn't believe that the reason we were crossing Wyoming, at a time when the Indians were angry, was because Ma meant to shoot Pa. But I did think that something hot was likely to happen at Fort Phil Kearny, if Pa was there. I didn't know what it would be but I wanted to hurry on to the fort, so Ma could get it over with.

"I don't care what they do as long as they don't make no more babies," G.T. said. "Keeping up with Marcy's about tuckered me out."

Three days after G.T. shot the antelope, with the sky spitting snow and the weather looking ugly, we found the first scalped man.

**4** MARCY found the dead miner while the rest of us were making camp. Uncle Seth decided he didn't like the tone of the weather, so he pulled up near a little grove of trees, where there was plenty of firewood and a little cover. Ma was rarely in the mood to quit early, but this time Uncle Seth persuaded her.

While we were all doing our chores, hobbling the mules, gathering firewood, getting out the blankets, and unpacking the cooking gear, Marcy came waddling up to the fire carrying an arrow.

"Now that's unusual," Uncle Seth said. "Indians aren't usually careless with arrows—it takes too long to make one. They will even pick up arrows off a busy battlefield. Where'd you get it, honey?"

At first Marcy just sulled. She could talk a little—

"mule" was one of her words, but usually she had to be coaxed before she'd come out with a word, and sometimes she wouldn't talk no matter how much we coaxed. Ma had wrapped up a few sticks of candy, back in Omaha—I believe she was saving them for Christmas—but she had no intention of using them to bribe Marcy into telling us where she picked up the arrow.

"I am not fool enough to bribe a child," Ma said. "She'll come out with it when she thinks it's the only way to get attention."

Ma was right. Marcy sulled for a few minutes and then led us right to the dead miner—a sight none of us had been expecting to see, just before supper. The man's head had been pounded in with his own spade; his eyes were missing and his legs had been split to the bone. A big patch of hair had been ripped off the front part of his head, which was black with blood. The dead miner was naked— no sign of his clothes anywhere. It was only because of the bloody spade that we figured he was a miner. His stomach had been opened and most of his guts thrown to one side—the varmints had been into those, already.

I got to the corpse first. What was left didn't even look like a man. I thought for a moment that I had stumbled on the carcass of some strange Wyoming critter that I couldn't identify. Somehow it was his ears that convinced me that what lay exposed on the mountain meadow were the remains of a human being.

I guess G.T. felt just as confused.

"What's that?" he asked, when he first spied the body.

"Uh-oh," Uncle Seth said, when he saw the corpse. He tried to wave Ma and Neva off.

"You don't need to see this, Mary Margaret," he said. "Neva don't either."

Ma ignored the comment and walked right around him.

"Whoa!" he said to Neva, but she walked around him too.

Then we all looked at the dead man for a while, in the thin failing light.

"Well, now I expect these young ones will have nightmares," Uncle Seth said. He was put out with Ma for ignoring his advice.

"Let 'em!" Ma said. "They've come all this way with us and they'll all be grown soon. Let them look at what happens when people get too mad to control themselves."

The snow began to fall, while we stood there looking at the dead miner. In a minute it covered the cavity in his belly and the bloody patch on his head.

"What did they do with his eyes?" Neva asked.

Nobody had an opinion. Ma took Marcy by the hand and walked back to start the cooking.

I remembered all the miners we had seen tramping along, while we were traveling by the Platte.

"Some people must want to get rich bad," I said.

"Yes, they do," Uncle Seth said.

"Not me," G.T. said. "Not me, not me, not me."

"Let's get him buried, before the ground freezes," Uncle Seth said.

We got a spade and a pickax from the wagon—none of us much wanted to use the miner's own spade. Soon we had a pretty good grave. Ma called us to eat before we quite got finished—she had stewed up some of G.T.'s antelope. We lowered the man into his grave, but the stew was ready before we covered him up. Somehow just thinking about him hiked our appetites.

After supper Uncle Seth took a lantern and went back himself to cover up the dead traveler.

"Do you want to say a scripture?" he asked Ma.

"The grass withereth, the flower fadeth," Ma said. "You boys go cut some more wood—the chill's coming. We're going to need a good fire tonight."

G.T. and I chopped firewood from the little grove, while Uncle Seth shoveled clods over the dead miner. G.T.'s hands were so cold that he did a poor job of hobbling our mule Montgomery, who got away during the night.

The next morning, half a mile away, we found Montgomery dead—he was almost as messed up as the miner.

"Cougar," Uncle Seth said. "I expect when we strike Fort Reno we better bargain for another mule."

"Damn that Montgomery!" G.T. said. He was miserable all day—the death of our mule had been his fault.

**5** I FOUND the second dead miner while following a deer near a little copse of trees—I wanted to get that deer, to show G.T. he wasn't the only one who could shoot. The miner's body was on the bald prairie, with an arrow stuck in the ground beside it, like a signpost.

I was nearly a mile from the wagon when I stumbled on the body, which was even more cut up than the first corpse. It was cold—the body sparkled with frost. It didn't look human, any more than the first one had. The face was all smashed in, but the eyes hadn't been removed: they were staring up, like frosted crystals, into the sky. A patch of scalp was gone, and so were the man's privates. Both legs had been split open and his tongue had been cut out.

I stopped dead, when I saw that corpse. The hair

on my head stood up—I couldn't control it. The grove of trees wasn't fifty yards away—it was right there, dense and dark. Whoever killed the miner might be right there, watching me. I wanted to turn and run for the wagon, which was just over the swell of the prairie, getting farther away every minute.

Then the deer I was following stopped too, just shy of the woods. It stood in plain view—it seemed to be staring into the woods. Maybe it saw the Indian who had killed the miner—maybe it smelled an Indian, or a bunch of Indians.

The deer suddenly turned broadside to me, making such an easy target that I aimed, shot, and killed it. I felt that I either had to steady myself and shoot that deer, or else scream and run off. I shot, and the deer fell, perfectly dead. Usually a deer, even one hit solid, will jump around a little, or run a few yards before giving up its life; but this deer just dropped.

It was a small deer, smaller than G.T.'s antelope. I felt I could probably carry it to the wagon, or at least drag it close enough that someone would see me and come help.

But the fear inside me had me paralyzed. I couldn't step around the dead miner to go get the deer. What was in my mind was that if I went a foot closer to the trees I would end up with my head smashed in and my privates cut off; there would only be a patch of blood where my hair was.

I don't know what I would have done—it was my good luck that Uncle Seth heard the shot and came loping over on Sally to help me.

"Venison, that's fine," he said, when I pointed to the dead deer.

Then he looked down and saw the corpse.

"Uh-oh," he said. "This is getting repetitious. Let me see the arrow.

"It's a Sioux arrow, same as the one Marcy found," he said. "If Charlie or Villy were here they could probably tell us what band it came from. I've not had a proper opportunity to study Sioux arrows, myself."

Ma and Neva didn't come look, this time. The ground was frozen so hard we couldn't get a real grave dug. We put the miner in a shallow trench and piled rocks on until we had it pretty solidly covered.

"An antelope beats a deer, anytime," G.T. said.

"Yes, and there's something that beats an antelope," Uncle Seth said, pointing to a half dozen brown dots, far up the valley.

"Buffalo!" Neva said. "It's about time we seen some."

At first I could hardly believe the brown dots were buffalo. Pa and Uncle Seth had talked to me all through my childhood about buffalo, and yet these were the first we'd seen. Even now, the fact that they were so few was disappointing.

"It's only six," I said.

"Maybe if I'm lucky I can bring one down," Uncle Seth said.

He wasn't lucky, though. Long before he came upon the buffalo they took fright and rumbled over a ridge, into another valley, where Uncle Seth didn't seem to think it wise to follow them.

Ma noticed his caution and taxed him about it when he came back.

"Why'd you pull up?" she asked.

"The bufs had too big a lead," he said.

Ma didn't press him, but that night she raised a question that had been in my mind all day, ever since I stumbled on the second miner.

"Do you think they're watching us?" she asked.

Uncle Seth shook his head. "If you mean Indians, no," he said.

"Why wouldn't they be?" Ma asked. "This is their country. They were watching those two miners who got chopped up."

"Maybe not," Uncle Seth said. "It might not be a tribe or a band that's doing this. It might just be a lone warrior who don't like miners."

"If they're watching us, would you know it?" Ma asked.

"The Indians out here ain't shy," he told her. "If they wanted to come out and inspect us, they would. Remember the Pawnees, and the Bad Faces? If the Sioux or the Cheyenne wanted to come out and inspect us, they would, even if all they wanted was to bargain for a little tobacco."

That seemed reasonable to me—I don't know what Ma thought, but she and Uncle Seth sat up talking, now and then throwing wood on the fire, until real late. I couldn't hear what they were talking about, but just the fact that they were talking pleasantly made it easier to go to sleep.

**6** T H E next day we reached Fort Reno and managed to purchase a large brown mule, to take the place of Montgomery. Ma objected to the trade—we still had four mules and a horse, which she thought was ample, but Uncle Seth bought the brown mule over her objections.

"They've got more transport animals than they can feed, at this fort—this mule was a bargain," he said. "I say we name him Reno, after the fort he's leaving."

In fact, Fort Reno seemed to be a foul place, full of soldiers who were drunk and scared. Some of the soldiers stared at Ma and Neva as if they had never seen a woman or a girl before—their stares were impolite, the more so because all the soldiers were filthy.

"We don't bathe much, when it's chilly," the

quartermaster explained. He was a skinny corporal with a wheezing cough who claimed that hardly a day passed without some patrol finding a dead miner or two on the prairie trails.

"If you've found two, that makes sixteen," he said. "Sixteen dead is a lot of dead—the army ought never to have put up these forts if they can't protect the roads any better than that."

"Why, it would take a thousand soldiers to protect this route," Uncle Seth said. "I doubt the army can afford to allow a thousand soldiers to loiter around in a place like this."

Ma asked about Pa and was told he was at Fort Phil Kearny, hauling wood—the news made her impatient to leave, but the new mule, not knowing any of our mules, was jumpy and took a while to harness.

In the center of the fort, not far from where the mules were stabled, there was a wagon with a wooden cage in it. It looked empty, except for a pile of rags in the corner, but as we were getting ready to leave, the rags began to stir around and an old Indian man crawled out from under them. He was a terrible sight: naked, except for the rags he held around him, filthy, toothless, his hair full of straw and lint, his wrists bloody from a pair of handcuffs, blind or nearly blind. There seemed to be a film of some kind over one eye. While Uncle Seth was trying to get the new mule to accept the harness the old Indian man began to chant, in a high singsong voice. Pretty soon he was singing loud enough that everyone in the little fort could hear him.

Uncle Seth stopped what he was doing and stared at the old man for a while.

"Who *is* that?" he asked. "I swear he looks familiar."

The wheezy little quartermaster, whose name was Botchford, must have heard the old Indian's singing once too often, because he turned red in the face and began to threaten him with an iron from the smithy's forge.

"Shut up, you goddamn squeaker!" Botchford yelled—but the old man just went on chanting, as if Botchford wasn't there.

Botchford put the iron back in the forge—the color gradually left his face.

"I wish they'd hang him!" he said. "He's always making that racket."

Neva couldn't take her eyes off the old Indian in the cage.

"I wish I knew what he was singing," she said.

"Oh no you don't, young lady," Botchford said. "What's he's singing ain't for a young lady's ears."

Ma jumped in at that point, on Neva's side.

"I'm curious myself," she said. "What is the poor man saying?"

"Ma'am, it's just wild Indian preaching," Botchford said. "He's been preaching this wild Indian preaching all over the plains. It's got the tribes stirred up, which is why we caged him. They're sending him down to Fort Leavenworth until the tribes settle down."

"He's just one old man," Ma said. "What could he say that would be so bad?"

At that point Botchford got exasperated, partly with Ma and partly with the wild old prisoner. He began to stomp around and get red in the face again, as if the old man offended every belief he held.

"Oh, you want to know, do you?" he said. "All right then, you'll know. What he's saying is that a sheet of shit ten feet deep will cover the whole earth pretty soon, and all us whites will drown in it! Green shit! But the Indian folks can just dance on top of this shit! Then new grass is supposed to come out all over the world and all the dead buffalo will rise up and the Indians will rise up too, the dead ones and the living ones, Miniconjous and Cheyenne and the damned Blackfeet, and all the tribes will get to help themselves to the buffalo, without a single white person left to interfere with their feasting and whatever else they want to do."

After that speech Corporal Botchford was so out of breath that he sat down on an overturned bucket and glared at the old wild man in the cage.

"The Indians call him the Man of the Morning," he said, which caused Uncle Seth to perk up.

"Oh, that's him, by golly," he said. "He was way over at Fort Pierre the last time I saw him. Dick and I gave him a ride. He's aged a bunch since then."

"I guess he would, traveling all over the country, preaching his rant," Botchford said. "It's because of the likes of him that we've got sixteen chopped-up dead people scattered all over these plains."

The old man in the cage just went on chanting,

**7** T H E   farther north we went, the colder it got; in those days of bitter chill Uncle Seth's gimpy knee began to plague him. Some mornings Ma had to walk him around a little while, holding his arm, like you might do a lame horse, before he could get his knee to start working fairly well.

Once in a while we'd even hear him groan in his sleep. When he was awake he complained plenty, tracing the trouble all the way back to the day the Civil War started, although it had been the day after it ended when he accidentally shot himself.

"Seth, you can complain all the way back to Adam and it won't make you young again," Ma said. "You shot yourself in the knee, and that's that."

as if we didn't exist. The few Indians lazing around the fort didn't seem to be paying him any mind at all.

"Do you feed him?" Ma asked. "He looks pretty starved down."

"Not starved down enough!" the corporal said. "I'd hang him right now if it was my choice, but it ain't my choice."

"Why hang a preacher for preaching?" Ma asked. "I've heard plenty of white preachers say the same thing: the good dead will all be raised up to a new day, and the others will burn."

G.T. was getting spooked by all this talk of shit floods and the dead rising up.

"That's why I don't like sermons," he said. "I think it would be a better world if all the dead people just stayed in their graves, where it's comfortable."

"Give that old man some tobacco, Seth," Ma said.

"Hell, if you've got tobacco to spare, give *me* some," Corporal Botchford said. "I'm the fellow who just sold you a fine mule too cheap."

Uncle Seth gave them both a little tobacco. He even slipped the old Indian a little antelope jerky. When we rolled out of Fort Reno we could hear the Man of the Morning, still singing.

"I can see where listening to that all day might make a man jumpy," Uncle Seth said.

"It's just preaching, Seth," Ma said. "I despi that they've caged him like that."

What annoyed Ma most about it was that we weren't making very good time—the need to help Uncle Seth loosen up his knee every morning meant that we got off to a late start. Besides, we were in high country and it was already past the middle of December, which meant that we were traveling in the short days. It seemed as if the sun barely rose above the mountains before it started down again. Snow threatened nearly every day, and some days it did more than threaten. We saw no Indians, and no more buffalo, although Uncle Seth did kill a large cow elk, out of a herd we surprised one morning.

With the weather so sharp and the terrain unfamiliar, we didn't risk traveling after dark, so most days we couldn't make much more than ten miles.

At that we were lucky, I thought, because we were traveling a fairly smooth plain, with not too many humps or bumps in it. The mountains to the west looked too high to even think about crossing.

G.T. didn't like the mountains, or the thick forests on them, either.

"There could be a thousand bears, in a forest that thick," he said.

As we got closer to the fort where we were expecting to find Pa, everybody's mood got tense, except Ma's. She didn't seem to think it was anything out of the ordinary to plod along in the deeps of winter, in a country full of violent Indians, to find a man she hadn't seen in nearly two years. She was annoyed by delays, though, and was apt to speak sharply to anyone who didn't get their chores done quickly, in the mornings.

"If it was June you could loiter, but it ain't June," she pointed out.

It was clear to all of us that Uncle Seth wasn't nearly as eager to come on Pa as Ma was, even though Pa was his brother and his business partner.

"Dick Cecil does not like to be criticized, by women or anyone else," Uncle Seth remarked one night, while we were making supper off some of the cow elk he had killed. The meat was a little stringy, but it still beat mush.

Ma just gave him a mild look. It was clear that Pa's preference on that point didn't mean beans to her.

"I haven't come all this way to kiss his feet, if that's what you suppose," Ma said. "I have a few likes and dislikes of my own, you know."

"I speculate that it's mainly that Indian family of his that you don't like," Uncle Seth said.

Ma just shrugged, as if she were a little disgusted by his line of reasoning.

"Don't speculate," she said. "Mind your own business and I'll mind mine and Dick's.

"In some ways you have less sense than anybody I know," she added, after a pause.

"Now, that's a wild opinion if I ever heard one," Uncle Seth said.

"I wish we'd get to a fort," Neva said. "I'd like to hear someone play a fiddle or something. There's no excitement in this travel."

"I guess you'd be excited enough if some scalping Indians got after you," G.T. said.

The next day we saw our second grizzly. It was

about a mile away, across a snowy meadow, standing up on its hind legs, looking around.

"Get ready to shoot," G.T. urged Uncle Seth.

"Settle down," Uncle Seth said. "It's just a bear minding its own business. It hasn't given us any reason to shoot."

The bear never came any closer, or gave any reason to shoot, though we kept it in sight most of that day. It ambled along north, still about a mile away, as if it meant to keep us company at a comfortable distance.

"There would be nothing to keep it from sneaking in after dark and eating us all," G.T. said.

That night the moon shone unusually bright, so bright that it dimmed out the stars.

"It's getting toward the solstice," Uncle Seth observed. "Means winter's here. That bear we seen needs to be looking for itself a den."

The next morning was unusually cold. The mules' breath condensed in sizable clouds. Uncle Seth was a long time getting to his feet, even after Ma brought him three cups of coffee. In Fort Laramie we had all bought heavy gray coats, with hoods for our heads. I didn't wear mine often, because of the weight, but I wore it this morning and was glad to have it. Neva was the only one of us who seemed to like the cold.

"I'd like to go where it's colder than this," she said. "I'd like to go clean to the pole."

"You may get your wish, the way this weather feels," Uncle Seth said.

Although all of us knew, in our heads, that we

were traveling to a certain place, to look for a certain person, we had been rolling on for so long that it seemed that rolling on was just our life, now. The old life we had had in Boone's Lick seemed far away, not just across distance but across time too. I could hardly imagine going back there and having a stopped life again.

That wasn't the way Ma seen it, of course. For us it might be a new way of life, but for her it had a plain purpose.

"Think we'll make it by Christmas, Seth?" she asked, when we finally set off, that cold day.

"I sure do," Uncle Seth said. "I think we're close enough that we could run into a patrol any day."

The words were scarcely out of his mouth before Neva began to point.

"There's a fort!" she said. "Is that it?"

Neva had by far the best eyes in the family. I looked, but I couldn't see anything.

"Is she seeing things?" Uncle Seth asked.

Ma was staring too.

"It seems like I see something," she said. "Is it a fort?"

"Fort, fort, fort!" Marcy said. She was at the stage where she could repeat any word she heard.

"I believe she's right, Seth," Ma said. "I believe it *is* a fort."

"Is it the right fort, Seth?" Ma asked, when we were close enough that we could all see it.

"It sure is—we've arrived!" he said.

"Pa, Pa, I see him," Neva said. "That's him with an axe, standing by that wood wagon."

"You must have been an eagle in your other life, Neva," Ma said. "I can't see him yet."

"Right there, right there!" Neva said, pointing.

She was excited at being the first one to spot Pa.

She was right, too. It *was* Pa, and he *was* standing by a wood wagon, with an axe in his hand. The only thing Neva didn't notice at first—I guess because of excitement—was the young Indian woman standing beside Pa, big with child.

**8** S E E I N G  our wagon come creaking up to Fort Phil Kearny that morning must have given Pa one of the biggest shocks of his life.

At first he didn't seem to notice us, or think anything out of the ordinary was happening. I suppose he thought we were just one more wagon full of hopefuls, on our way to the gold fields up the Bozeman Trail. A couple of other woodcutters were sitting with their backs to the wagon wheels, sharpening their axes—I believe Pa was trying to josh one of them into sharpening his, when we approached.

What he missed at first glance he saw plain enough on the second: his own mules, his own wagon, his brother, his own children, and—particularly—his own wife.

You can bet that we were the last people Pa expected to see, coming up that prairie road to the fort. In his mind I'm sure he had us way back down the Missouri River, at Boone's Lick—when his eyes finally told him his mind was way off track, he didn't want to believe it at first. He blinked two or three times and looked off—then he looked at us again, as if we were just a mirage that would vanish once he got a better look at it.

When we were only about forty yards away and he had to admit to himself that he wasn't seeing any mirage, he just looked stumped for a minute, blank, and then his face darkened and we could all see his temper rising. That was Pa's way: it never took him long to go from being stumped to being mad.

The young Indian woman with the swelling belly must have learned something about Pa's moods by that time: the minute his face changed she went scurrying like a doe through the gates of the fort. Big belly or not, she moved quickly.

The woodchoppers who were sharpening their axes hadn't noticed Pa's change in mood—at least, they hadn't until he dropped his axe and came charging out to meet us.

"I believe he's mad as a bear," G.T. said.

Ma didn't say anything, and neither did Uncle Seth.

Neva wasn't scared of anything, not even Pa. She *had* noticed the Indian woman's belly, of course.

"I wonder if I've got any more half sisters, up here at this fort," she said.

"I'd ask your Pa, if I were you," Ma said. "I hope he's kept count, at least."

Our skittish new mule, Reno, must have thought Pa was as mad as a bear, because he tried to bite him when Pa walked up and stopped the team.

Pa just whacked him one—he had no use for impertinent mules.

"What in the hell is *this,* Mary Margaret?" Pa asked, spitting mad.

"Why, can't you see, Dick? It's your family," Ma said.

"Your *Missouri* family, that is," she added. "I realize you've got a few others. We hadn't seen you in such a spell we just decided to pay you a Christmas visit."

Ma was perfectly cool—it startled Pa a little. He may have forgotten how cool Ma was in a storm— or it may be that he just wasn't used to people who didn't seem to care that he was mad.

"Seth, goddamnit, what *is* this?" Pa asked. "Who said you all could come here? You oughtn't to have allowed it."

"I *didn't* allow it," Uncle Seth said. "It happened despite me. I've done nothing but argue against it mile by mile, all the way from Boone's Lick, Missouri. But here we are."

There was silence for a minute.

"It's my opinion that shooting Mary would have been the only way to stop her, and I wasn't up to shooting her," Uncle Seth said.

Neva had no use for family arguments—anyway

she scarcely knew Pa, and she was eager for company, so she jumped off the wagon and marched right over to where the woodchoppers sat. In no time she had struck up a conversation with them.

"Seth's right," Ma said "He would have had to shoot me to stop me, and he wasn't up to shooting me. Would *you* have been up to shooting me, Dick?"

Although still plenty mad, Pa seemed a little off balance. Even though he was standing only a few feet from Ma and Uncle Seth—just far enough back that the new mule couldn't bite him—I think part of him still didn't believe his family had actually showed up in Wyoming. Some little part of him must have still thought it was a dream he ought to be waking up from, anytime. He looked at Uncle Seth again, and this time he didn't sound so fierce.

"There must be some way to stop a woman, rather than let her drag a wagon and a bunch of kids all this way," he said. "You could have hog-tied her and left her in the cellar."

"We don't have a cellar," Ma reminded him.

"Well, then the stables or somewhere," Pa said. He seemed confused—I think he was losing steam by the minute. I was even beginning to feel a little sorry for Pa—I don't know about G.T., who had got off on the wrong foot with Pa years before by losing a good pocketknife Pa had given him, which got him such a thrashing that he had been leery of Pa ever since.

With Uncle Seth watching, Ma climbed off the

wagon seat and marched over to Pa, looking him up and down from a short distance away. Something about her stance made Uncle Seth nervous.

"Maybe the children and I better go on into the fort and see if they can spare a little fodder for the livestock," Uncle Seth said.

"You stay put," Ma said.

"I was just thinking you might want privacy," Uncle Seth said. He was getting more and more nervous—and so was I.

"Seth, shut up," Ma said. "Don't talk and don't move. This will just take a minute."

"A minute?" Uncle Seth said. "After traveling all these months?"

"Some things take months, and other things just take a minute," Ma said.

She turned back to Pa.

"You're not making me feel welcome, Dick—although I'm your wife," Ma said. "Am I welcome, or ain't I?"

"Did I ask you to come—no!" Pa said. "So you're not welcome. I expect you knew that before you left home, you independent hussy."

"I *did* know it before I left home but I wanted to hear it from you," Ma said.

"Why?"

"Because I'm not the sort of woman to quit a man through the mails," Ma said. "I can only quit a man face-to-face, and right here and now I'm quitting you."

Marcy woke from a nap. She didn't see Ma, so she raised a wail.

"Good Lord, you even brought the baby?" Pa said.

"Yes, the child you've never seen," Ma said. "You understood me, didn't you, Dick? We're quits."

Annoyed as he was with Ma, those words were not quite what Pa had been expecting.

"We're quits? That seems hasty, Mary Margaret," he said.

That must have been the wrong thing to say, because Ma colored up and gave him a roundhouse slap that would have floored any man less tall and stout than Pa.

"Not hasty, tardy—tardy by sixteen years!" Ma said.

Then she got back in the wagon, took the reins from Uncle Seth, and drove us into Fort Phil Kearny, leaving Pa standing by himself, rubbing his sore jaw.

**9** M A never explained why she did what she did that cold evening in Wyoming— for it was nearly dark when we reached the fort. The bright moon, not quite full, came up not much later.

To Ma, I guess, the matter spoke for itself. She had pulled us out of our lives and traveled hundreds of miles across the west, to tell Pa she was quitting him. She seemed to feel it was something she owed him. She did what she came to do, and that was that.

It shocked Pa, and it shocked Uncle Seth, who didn't seem to be particularly out of sorts with his brother—but Ma quitting Pa didn't really make much difference to the rest of the family. Marcy was too young to notice, Neva was trying to get the woodchoppers to arrange a dance, or at least some fiddle music, and as soon as we got in the fort, Pa's Indian wife, who had two toddlers besides the one in her belly, presented G.T. with a little brown puppy, which started to lick his face. The puppy soon attached himself to G.T. like a leech. G.T. was too taken with the puppy to give much thought to what happened between Pa and Ma.

I think Pa's little Indian wife—he called her Sweetbreads—probably saw that we were tired and hungry and gave us the puppy to eat; but G.T. took to it so that after five minutes no one would have dared to try and eat it.

I was the only one, it seemed, who took much note of what had just happened between Pa and Ma. Had she really brought us all this way just to tell him she was quitting him?

I believe the same question occurred to Uncle Seth. As we were finding a spot to park our wagon, inside the stockade, he looked at Ma kind of funny.

"Did you really come all this way just to tell Dick you were quitting him?" he asked. "If that was all you had to tell him, you could have sent me with the news."

Ma looked a little exasperated by that comment—she hadn't completely cooled down.

"No, Seth—I didn't send you because I'm *keeping* you!" she said. "Or would you rather just live out here and run wild, like your brother?"

"Not me," Uncle Seth said at once. "Not me. I'm so used to you now I wouldn't know what to do without you."

"That's right, you wouldn't!" Ma said sharply.

"I believe I will just go see Dick for a minute, though," Uncle Seth said. "I'd like to find out if the business is prospering."

"Go—Sherman can stable these mules," Ma said.

I *did* stable the mules, with the help of G.T. and a couple of friendly young soldiers, who seemed fairly nervous—there had been rumors of an Indian attack, they said. Colonel Carrington, who was in charge of the fort, had never fought Indians in his life, which, in the soldiers' opinion, meant that he wasn't taking the threat seriously enough.

I knew nothing about the matter, of course—I wasn't too worried about Indians yet, probably because I still had the business of Pa and Ma on my mind. I was beginning to get the notion that Ma might even want to *marry* Uncle Seth. Could *that* be why she quit Pa? And if it wasn't *that*, could it be because of one of the little things, such as his two Indian families, or the fact that he only showed up in Missouri for a few days every year or two? I didn't know—I never *did* know—but I turned the whole business over in my mind many times. It was such unfamiliar territory that I could not even be sure I knew the difference between a big thing and a little thing, where Ma was concerned.

Though that moment—the moment when Ma slapped Pa, first with words and then with her hand—lodged in my mind for years, I didn't get to puzzle it over much at the time because we had barely got the mules unhitched and settled for the night before Ma had a set-to with that rude Colonel Fetterman, whom we had met in Fort Laramie. The set-to occurred just as the flag was being lowered for the evening, and resulted in our getting expelled from the fort for the night.

I don't know how the quarrel started—by the time I heard voices rising and turned around to see Colonel Fetterman, in a pitch of rage, pointing his finger at Ma, the battle was on.

"Get out! Get out! Get this damn woman out of the fort!" he yelled, addressing himself to the little detail of soldiers who were lowering the flag.

The soldiers were stunned by this sudden command—they had been happy to see us. Stuck off as they were in a remote little fort, not too many new faces came their way. Neva had already made herself popular—though there was no fiddle in sight, one soldier had dug out a harmonica and was making music for her already.

"Colonel Fetterman, what is the problem?" one of the young lieutenants stammered out.

"You dare to talk to me like that! . . . Military matters!" Colonel Fetterman yelled. He was pointing his finger at Ma, despite the fact that he had on white gloves.

"Stop that, sir! Don't you know it's rude to point?" Ma said.

"I will not have a treasonous woman in this fort—get 'em out! Get 'em out!" Colonel Fetterman said. "We'll cage our Indians any way we want to, and your opinion be damned!"

Then he stomped off.

The young officer looked deeply embarrassed.

"I don't know what to say, ma'am," he said. "I fear you'd best leave."

"What? Is that fool the boss of this fort?" Ma asked.

"No—Colonel Carrington's in charge—I suppose you could appeal to him," the young man said.

There was a silence.

"You don't seem to think I *should* appeal to Carrington, though," Ma said. "Is that correct?"

"Colonel Carrington dislikes trouble of any kind," the young soldier said. "In fact, he dislikes being disturbed at all, when it's this late in the evening."

"Does he dislike Colonel Fetterman?" Ma asked.

The young lieutenant looked even more embarrassed.

"Now you've put me on the spot, ma'am," he said.

The string bean of a corporal who was folding up the flag wasn't as timid as the lieutenant.

"No, Carrington don't like Fetterman—nobody likes Fetterman. He has abused me more than once," the corporal said. "But if I were you I'd just go camp outside tonight—the air's fresher, anyway. There's a passel of smelly old people in this fort, I can tell you."

"Good advice—get the mules, Sherman," Ma said. "G.T., give Marcy that puppy and help your brother pack up. I believe I'd feel cramped in here anyway, just from knowing Colonel Fetterman is around."

Luckily we hadn't unpacked much gear. The soldiers, all of them disappointed that we were leaving so soon, were quick to help rehitch the mules.

When we rolled out of the stockade Pa and Uncle Seth were sitting on the back end of one of the wagons, talking. If Pa was still disturbed by what had occurred, he didn't show it.

"Hell, you just went in and now you're coming out," Pa said, hopping off the wagon. "Didn't you like our nice little fort?"

"Yes, but it's too small for Colonel Fetterman and me both," Ma said.

"Oh, that goddamn whippersnapper," Pa said, as if the mere mention of Colonel Fetterman explained everything.

Pa seemed friendly—so friendly I was hoping he would come over and camp with us. Being the oldest, I had spent more time with Pa than the other children—I suspect I missed him most. I would have liked to hear about some of his adventures, out in the west.

But he didn't camp with us. When full dark came he went inside the fort, to his Indian wife Sweetbreads and his two button-eyed toddlers. One of the cooks had pressed some porridge on Ma, while we were in the fort, so we ate porridge, with a little molasses the cook had given her. I guess that molasses was the sweetest thing Marcy had ever tasted. I believe she would have drunk a quart of it, if we'd had it.

"What did you say to set the colonel off?" Uncle
Seth inquired.

"I complained about the way the army caged
that old Indian, back at the last fort," Ma said.

The only one missing was Neva, who probably
danced all night with the soldiers. G.T. and his
puppy had a tug-of-war with a sock. Ma and Uncle
Seth sat up late, talking. It felt odd to be camping
so close to Pa—I couldn't get him off my mind,
couldn't sleep, and sat up and watched the bright
moon until it was almost dawn.

**10** T H E next morning the smell of bacon brought me out of a deep drowse. It had snowed a little during the night, not much—just enough that we had to be careful to shake out our blankets. While I was warming my hands around a coffee cup Pa came driving his wagon our way, with five or six wood wagons behind him. He stopped the team for a minute and came tramping over, through the light snow.

"Morning, travelers," he said. "What's your plans?"

"Why would you need to know?" Ma asked.

"I want to borrow our whelps, for a day, that's why," Pa said. "I'll take them out with the wood train and see how they perform with a saw and an axe. A good day's work won't hurt 'em—they might even like it."

"You can come too, Seth, if you're a mind," Pa said.

"No, Dick—I prefer to avoid the saw and the axe," Uncle Seth said. "Besides, it wouldn't do to leave Colonel Fetterman unguarded, while Mary Margaret is around. If he was to cross her I expect she'd tear his throat out."

"Just so it's *his* throat, not mine," Pa said.

Ma was watching Pa—I couldn't tell what her attitude was.

"I believe I done you a favor by quitting you, Dick," she said. "Now you won't have to drag yourself all the way down to Missouri, every year or two, to make me a baby. You can make a passel of them right here in Wyoming, without the expense of travel."

Pa had a pleasant expression on his face, and it didn't change. He just pretended Ma hadn't said anything. When he did speak it was only about the weather.

"The fort Indians say there's a blizzard coming," he said. "They know their business, when it comes to weather. It might be best if you stayed near the fort for a day or two, before you go traipsing back across the baldies."

"Who mentioned going back?" Ma asked. "We might be planning to go north and strike gold, for all you know."

"I doubt you'll strike gold but you might strike the Cheyenne," Pa said. "Hurry it up, Sherman."

Of course, G.T. and I were eager to go with Pa, and Ma didn't forbid it, though I don't think she was too keen on the prospect.

"You wouldn't be trying to steal my boys, would you, Dick?" she asked, when we were dragging our big gray coats over to the wood wagon. If the blizzard came we meant to be prepared.

"Just for the day, Mary Margaret," Pa said. "We've got a wood train to fill before that blizzard arrives. There's no reason to let two big strapping boys sit idle, that I can see."

Ma looked a little stiff, but she raised no objections.

"I hate to leave my puppy," G.T. said, as we were hurrying over to the wood wagons. But he didn't say it loud enough for Pa to hear.

# 11

"Y O U boys are lucky, that mother of yours has got snap!" Pa said, as he led the wood train northeast of the fort, toward the thick forests that covered the mountains.

I thought the remark odd—after all, he was the man who had been married to Ma for sixteen years—it wasn't as if she were a distant cousin, or just some stranger he had met in passing. Why would Pa talk about Ma as if she were just someone he admired, in a distant way?

I didn't know—I still don't—because we arrived at our place of work and had to jump out and start unloading the saws and axes. It was plain from all the stumps and wood chips all over the place that the woodchoppers had been working on the clump of trees for several days.

After watching us try to use axes for a few minutes, Pa changed his mind and assigned us to the big crosscut saw.

"You're way off in your skills with the axe," Pa said. "Seth ought to be ashamed of himself, for not teaching you better. You're either going to cut your own foot off, or one of somebody else's, which won't do. Try the saw. It will spare the company a lost foot or two."

I was chastened, and so was G.T. We had fancied ourselves the equal of any man, when it came to chopping firewood, but watching the other woodcutters soon put an end to that illusion. All the other woodcutters were faster and more accurate—of course, they used axes all day every day, while all we did was break up a little firewood for the campfire, when there was wood to be had.

Cold as it was, working with a crosscut saw on long lengths of pine log soon warmed both of us up. Before long we were down to our shirtsleeves, and were even thinking of taking off our shirts, as several of the woodchoppers had done. I don't know about G.T., but I was soon thinking thoughts that weren't entirely loyal to Ma, such as, why *not* live with Pa? The country was glorious—just being out in it was exciting, with the plains so vast and the mountains so high and adventure to be met with, every day.

Nothing of the sort could be said about Boone's Lick, or anywhere around it. There were no grizzly bears and no Indians—it had been a while since G.T. had even trapped a good mess of crawdads.

If we stayed and became woodcutters, like Pa, I

had no doubt we'd soon get the hang of the axes. And when there was no work to do, think of the hunting. We might find a place where there was still buffalo. We might slay a grizzly bear.

"Stay in rhythm, boys," Pa instructed. "Just be easy and stay in rhythm. Don't pull against one another."

He grabbed my end of the crosscut saw and was just demonstrating the proper pull when we all heard a *ti-yi*ing from the west and looked around to see about fifty Indians charging across the plain toward us.

"Whoa! Turn these wagons," Pa yelled—I have never seen men move quicker to obey an order. In two minutes the men had four of the wagons turned to form a square, with the other two outside it, to serve as bulwarks. There was already a fair amount of wood in the wagons, enough to provide some cover. I guess there were about twenty of us, all told, on the woodchopping detail—though the Indians had us outnumbered, we all had rifles. The situation didn't look hopeless.

Pa, though, seemed to take a cautious view. He was huddled down with a lanky old woodsman named Sam, the only man sawing who wore buckskin clothes.

"I expect they're just funning," Sam said.

The Indians had slowed up a little, but were still *ti-yi*ing.

"I hope so," Pa said. "It's too late to try and make for the fort."

"Oh, let's just shoot 'em," G.T. said.

"That might work if we had adequate ammunition," Pa said.

"Don't we?" I asked. I only had five shells myself but I figured Pa would have plenty.

Pa shook his head.

"The goddamn stingy army," he said. "We don't have much ammunition—the whole fort don't have much, for that matter."

All of a sudden a weak feeling came over me, much like the one that had come over me the day the grizzly bear charged. What had happened to the dead miners might be about to happen to us. Missouri began to look a lot better to me, crawdads or no crawdads.

"Don't shoot, they may be funning!" Pa yelled, but despite Pa's clear instructions the woodchoppers soon began to fire at the Indians, who were riding around us in a big circle, still *ti-yi*ing.

"Stop shooting, damnit! They're still out of range," Pa yelled again.

I guess he was right. The Indians looked close, like the grizzly bear had looked big, but they weren't close—unless the woodcutters were all bad shots. Not a single Indian fell, or even ducked. A few of them had guns and popped at us a few times—four or five others, showing off, I guess, raced into bow-and-arrow range and let fly. Most of the arrows just thunked into the wood wagons, though one axman got hit in the leg.

"We're in plain sight of the fort," Sam observed. "I expect they'll send out a relief force, if these boys will just be patient."

Neither Sam nor Pa had fired a shot, or even raised their guns.

"I wish I had a spyglass—damn it, why did I come off without one!" Pa said. He wasn't paying the whooping, yipping Indians much mind. Instead he seemed to be trying to see into the forests.

"You think there's more?" Sam asked.

"There could be," Pa said. "There could be lots more."

"Doubt it," Sam said. "The Sioux will rarely hold an ambush. The Cheyenne either—their young braves get too impatient to be in on the fight."

"We could try for the fort," Sam suggested, after a while.

"They'd be on us like weasels on a squirrel," Pa said. "We're safest right where we are."

Just then it began to cloud over—I thought of Uncle Seth and his beliefs about bad things happening in cloudy weather.

The Indians who were harassing us began to yell even louder and to make insulting gestures—two or three of the woodchoppers continued to pop at them, but so far we hadn't hit a single one.

"I hope that relief Sam was talking about gets here pretty soon," G.T. said.

It was a comfort that we could see the fort—the back side of it, anyway—but from where we crouched, behind our wagons, it looked about fifty miles distant. What if everyone was in the mess hall, eating porridge with molasses, and hadn't noticed that we were under attack? Maybe they were all so busy eating and cussing that they hadn't even heard the shooting.

"This is the last time I ever come woodcutting with only four shells for my gun," Pa said. "If the damn army can't spare us no more ammunition than that, I believe I'll just stay in."

By then most of the woodcutters had shot up all their ammunition, and yet no Indians were dead. The woodcutters stood holding their useless rifles —they all looked scared.

Then six or seven more Indians came loping into the valley from the far end. They *ti-yi*ed a little, but they didn't join the party that had us trapped. They were nearly naked, and all painted up, but they seemed in an idle mood. One got off and examined one of his horse's hooves. The others rode off and left him. The Indian with the sore-footed horse gathered up a few sticks and began to build a little fire.

"Sam, I'm getting a bad suspicion," Pa said. "You know how sometimes you can kind of *feel* Indians, if there's a bunch of them around close?"

Sam just nodded his head.

"I'm feeling Indians," Pa said. "I'm feeling *lots* of Indians! Damn, I regret not bringing my spyglass!"

Just then we heard a bugle, though we could see no soldiers. There was a kind of ridge between us and the troops—it was called Lodgepole Ridge, though I didn't know that until much later.

As soon as they heard the bugle about half the Indians that had been circling us pulled off and went over to the little group that had just loped into the valley.

The warrior with the sore-footed horse was all by himself, warming himself by his little fire.

Then the cavalry began to pour over the little ridge, with a bugler and a flag and Colonel Fetterman in the lead—I recognized him by his white gloves.

"The goddamn fool, don't he see that it's a trap!" Pa yelled.

I thought he'd be happy that relief was finally coming, but he wasn't happy. He began to jump up and down on the wagon, waving his arms and yelling for the soldiers to go back.

Of course, they were a mile or two away—they couldn't hear him. Even if they had, it's not likely Colonel Fetterman would pay much attention to a woodcutter.

The six or seven Indians who had just loped up the valley took fright when they saw the cavalry— they hit out across the valley for the nearest trees.

Only the lone Indian with the sore-footed horse didn't seem concerned. He scattered his little fire and hopped on his horse, watching the soldiers for a minute before he went trotting off.

"Decoys! Decoys! That's all they are," Pa said, jumping off the wagon. "Hasn't the damn fool been in the army long enough to learn about decoys?"

"Hey, what's the army doing?" G.T. asked. "They're supposed to rescue us."

That had been my opinion too—and even the

opinion of the Indians who were harassing us—the minute they saw the cavalry most of them began to peel off toward the woods.

Maybe Colonel Fetterman *had* meant to rescue us, when he left the fort, but the sight of those decoy Indians swayed his judgment. The cavalrymen had been moving along at a slow gallop, but then the bugler blew the charge. I guess the colonel thought he could cut those few Indians off before they reached the woods.

In a minute the cavalry was in full charge, headed for the Indian with the sore-footed horse— only his horse made a quick recovery and was soon outrunning the soldiers.

"The oldest trick, the wounded bird," Pa said.

The cavalry was deep in the valley now, but they weren't catching the Indians, who were on fine quick horses.

"Look, Sam," Pa said.

"Oh, Lord," Sam said.

"Oh, dern," G.T. said.

The woods on every side began to boil with movement—I wasn't sure what was happening, at first. There was so much snow kicked into the air that I thought it might mean some kind of avalanche, caused by a buffalo herd that had decided to pass through.

But it was all Indians, hundreds of Indians, maybe thousands, and the war cries they screamed as they plunged into battle nearly scared my scalp off, and G.T.'s too. In nightmares I still hear those war cries today.

In a minute the Indians had closed around the cavalrymen—the few cavalrymen who tried to re-treat were quickly cut down. There were so many arrows in the air that they made a cloud. I even saw a crow fall—it had just been flying low over the valley and suddenly found itself stuck with arrows.

"We better go, while they're busy," Pa said, crawling up on the wagon seat.

"Oh, they don't want *us,*" Sam said.

That seemed to be true—the Indians who had been circling us pulled away to join the general bat-tle; guns were popping all over the valley, arrows and lances skewered men on the run, while others got hacked down with hatchets.

"No, they don't want us, but the frenzy's on them," Pa said. "They might not be able to stop killing. Some of the young warriors might want a few more easy scalps."

Most of the woodchoppers were like frozen men, staring at what was happening in the valley below. The cavalry had long since been scattered into many groups, pockets of five or six men, all fight-ing for their lives and losing—falling.

Even Sam seemed frozen by the spectacle.

"I would never have expected Indians to hold an ambush this well," he said.

"Well, they're learning," Pa said. "Come on, boys—whip up! Now's our chance, if we've got a chance."

The woodchoppers came unfrozen and we began a wild race for the fort. I suppose the Indians might have loped over and killed us, if they'd noticed: our mules weren't capable of much speed. But there were some hardy soldiers in that troop of cavalry—a few of them forted up behind a little bump of rocks and put up stiff resistance. The Indians were ten deep around them, so it was hopeless, but while they were firing their last bullets or taking their last whacks with their sabers we flailed our team and rumbled back across that ridge, only to meet Ma and Uncle Seth, plunging along in the other direction.

Pa pulled up and stopped them, while the other wood wagons raced on to the fort.

"Stop, goddamnit! It's a massacre—are you crazy?" Pa yelled.

"No, but I've come for my boys, that you ought never to have taken off," Ma said.

"They're *my* boys too—I guess I'm allowed one day with them, even if it is a perilous day," Pa said.

"Quiet down, you two!" Uncle Seth said sharply. "This is no time for a family quarrel—it looks like the massacre's over."

Uncle Seth was right. Below us, across the valley, the Indians were going around, picking up rifles and pistols, pulling cartridge belts off soldiers, picking up arrows and hatchets, collecting their own dead. The ones who had taken all they could carry were already trailing away, into the woods.

In only a few minutes, every single Indian was gone; they melted right back into the forests that they had come racing out of.

"There may be a few wounded," Uncle Seth said. "It would be unusual for every last man to be killed stone dead, in a fracas like this."

"Let's go," Ma said.

"Go where?" Uncle Seth asked.

"Go pick up the wounded," Ma said. "You just said there might be some."

"We might want to wait a few minutes, in case there are some young braves who aren't satisfied," Pa suggested. "It wouldn't be wise to tempt them."

"But the wounded might die," Ma said. "These Indians just killed a whole army—I doubt they'd bother with a scrawny bunch like us."

"Where's Marcy?" G.T. asked. "Where's my pup?"

"Left with wife number three—is that the right number, Dick?" Ma asked, giving him a look.

"Close enough," Pa said. "Why don't you take the youngsters back to the fort—me and Seth can gather up the wounded, if any."

"No, it might require two wagons," Ma said. "Besides, Seth's so gimpy he's worthless, in this chill weather."

"It's going to be a bad sight, Mary Margaret," Pa said. "You don't have to see it."

"I'm a woman who's buried four sons—by myself," Ma said. "Bad sights don't affect me."

Pa turned his wagon and said no more.

**12** W E took our two wagons down into that valley of death, to search for the wounded among the dead, but there was not a single wounded man—not one. Though the fight had lasted only a half hour at most, the Indians had managed to do the same things to Colonel Fetterman's troop that they had done to the miners we had found back on the trail. Eyes were gouged out, guts spilled, privates cut off, legs split, faces smashed in. Some of the bodies were naked, some not.

Colonel Fetterman's body was leaning against one of the rocks, on the little outcropping. His throat had been cut and it looked as if he might have taken a few licks to the head, but he wasn't torn up as badly as some of his men.

If Ma remembered that she had once told Colonel Fetterman that if he had eighty men to put at risk he would probably lose every one of them, she never mentioned it—but it had turned out to be an accurate prophecy: eighty cavalrymen died that day, on the field beyond Lodgepole Ridge.

Pa and Uncle Seth checked every corpse, to be sure it *was* a corpse, but we didn't remove the bodies. We only had two wagons, and Pa was nervous besides.

"That many Indians could take this fort," he said. "I have never seen that many Indians in one force, and Sam hasn't, either. I doubt there's bullets enough in the magazine to hold them off, if they come at us. A victory like this will surely pump them up."

"I expect we better bunk in the fort tonight, then," Uncle Seth said. "Colonel Fetterman won't be there to throw Mary out."

Already, because of the chill, the dead cavalrymen had stiffened—all over the field we could see legs and arms sticking up. Of course, growing up during the Civil War I had heard many stories of the hundreds and thousands that died at Gettysburg, Chancellorsville, Vicksburg, and the other great battles. Eighty dead would have been the result of just a small skirmish, in that war.

But we had seen these eighty dead men ride over the ridge that morning, in the full glory of their lives, racing down on their foe like cavalrymen are supposed to—and now they were all dead and stiff, their limbs sticking out at crazy angles—I felt like

I was seeing all the dead, of all the wars, not just these few poor soldiers.

Pa and Uncle Seth shot four or five badly wounded horses—the Indians had taken most of the rest, though a few had run off in panic and made it back to the fort.

Ma got down and walked among the bodies for a while, satisfying herself that they were all beyond our help.

"I'd hate to have a fault like this on my conscience," she said.

Not a man slept in Fort Phil Kearny that night—not unless it was Colonel Carrington, who we never glimpsed. Pa said this would ruin him, even if it had been Colonel Fetterman who led the reckless charge.

What interested *me* more was whether we would survive the night. Every man in the fort expected the Indians to attack, and the general view was that we lacked the ammunition to repel them.

Besides that, the fort Indians pointed out that tonight's moon would be a special moon—a power moon that the Sioux and the Cheyenne would want to take advantage of. They were right, at least about the power of the moon. The full moon that floated up into the sky that night was brighter than any lamp. A flare couldn't have lit the plains any brighter. Not a star was visible—the moon was too bright. It lit the prairies and shone into the forests where the Indians had hidden that day.

Every man in the fort stood in arms that night—only Neva, anxious for a dance, found the waiting boresome.

I don't know where all those Indians went, those hundreds of Sioux and Cheyenne; nobody knew, except themselves. But for whatever reason, they wasted the power moon, which shone all night with a brightness that I was never to experience again, not in my life.

Toward morning the wind rose, and it began to snow.

"Here comes that blizzard," Uncle Seth said.

"It's a shame they didn't bring in those bodies," Pa said. "Now we'll have to wait for a thaw."

The soldiers had been too scared, that day, to secure the bodies.

Still the moon shone—through its light we could see the heavy snowflakes, drifting down.

Ma stood on the parapet most of the night, with Pa and Uncle Seth. Someone had given her a rifle—she meant to fight if the Indians came. I had my rifle too. G.T. kept his puppy inside his big gray coat. Marcy was still with wife number three, Sweetbreads, as Pa called her.

By morning it was very cold—the wind was swirling the snow. Yet the moon was still visible, still bright. It had just transferred itself from one side of the sky to the other.

"It's shining for the dead—gone to their peace," Ma said.

We were invited into the mess hall for breakfast—the porridge with molasses sure tasted sweet.

**13** N E V A turned out to be the one who stayed in the west. She fought Ma and Pa and Uncle Seth to a standstill and stayed right there at Fort Phil Kearny, with Pa and Sweetbreads, or wife number three, as Ma always called her.

For Neva it was the beginning of a brilliant career—in no time she learned the Sioux language so well that the chiefs and generals began to take notice. At the big peace powwow in 1868, when the army knuckled under to Red Cloud and agreed to remove the three forts they had foolishly thrown up along the Bozeman, Geneva Cecil was the only interpreter that General Sherman trusted.

Then, before you could blink, Red Cloud, shifty as ever, stole Neva from General Sherman and hauled her all the way to New York City—she interpreted for him when he made his big speech at Cooper Union a year or two later. Her picture was in all the papers; I guess she did a crashing job.

Next thing we knew the great General Crook— Three Stars, or the Gray Fox to the red men—had enticed Neva away from Red Cloud; Crook kept her with him all the way to the Rosebud, where some intelligence she picked up from a Crow scout saved the testy general from a rout. All the military men said that if Custer had had her with him a week later she would have fought *him* to a standstill and helped him avoid his deadly blunder at the Little Bighorn.

We saw little of Neva in those years—she was always on the chase. Some say she left Crook to go marry her old admirer Wild Bill Hickok, but arrived too late to save him from drawing that famous dead man's hand, aces and eights, the hand he was studying when shot down by the coward McCall.

Then Buffalo Bill hired Neva for a while, to help pacify all the Indians who rode in his Wild West Show. I believe it was Neva who taught Sitting Bull to play Ping-Pong: there is even a picture of this.

From time to time Neva would marry: our count was three Indians, a gunfighter, two cowboys, and a trick roper—but she was bristly if we tried to get her to talk about her home life.

"What of it? Pa had more wives than I've had husbands," she insisted, if questioned.

Every two or three years someone would arrive from the dock or the railroad station with a small child for us—just a child with a note in Neva's hand.

"Ma, this is Ben—do your best, Neva," the note might say. Or, if the child happened to be a girl, the note would read: "Ma, this is Little Bat—good luck."

Uncle Seth would grumble about this practice— he claimed to be past the age when he could tolerate small children, but Ma raised all of Neva's offspring, to the number of six, never losing a one. Fortunately, thanks to the Black Hills gold rush, Pa and Uncle Seth prospered so in their hauling business that they sold out to the famous Wells Fargo Company; after that Ma didn't have to shoot horses out from under sheriffs to get vittles for her grandkids.

When General Crook was sent to Arizona to root out Geronimo he tried his best to get Neva to come with him, but she declined, on the grounds that fluency in Sioux didn't equip her to speak Apache. By then a young newspaperman named Hearst had hired her to write for his newspaper in San Francisco. The very year that Geronimo and his eighteen warriors came in, Neva published her famous book *The Western Avernus,* a story of how grievously we whites had mistreated the red man. The book sold millions of copies—at last count it had been translated into one hundred and three languages.

To her credit Neva devoted a lot of her time and energy to keeping up with Pa's Indian wives and his half-breed children. Her count, as to the children, was seventeen, spread among most of the tribes that had once held sway on the plains.

Pa never left the west—fortunately I was able to visit him often. G.T. took against him, on obscure grounds—it may have been that thrashing over the pocketknife—and never saw him again. The lumber business, which Pa went into after he and Uncle Seth sold out, proved to be Pa's doom, due to a freak accident in a sawmill he owned in Oregon. A big saw blade snapped, just at the wrong moment, and took Pa's head clean off. Neva buried him near The Dalles, a spot I have not visited—Neva assures me that his grave commands a glorious view of the Columbia River Gorge and the great country beyond it.

Ma and Uncle Seth were never parted. They quarreled their way through nearly fifty more years of life. A maiden aunt in Ohio left Uncle Seth a modest farm—before he could get around to selling it a handyman working on a fence punched a posthole a little too deep and struck oil. Uncle Seth was for selling the old place anyway, but Ma fought him like a tigress; she believed there was a future for oil, and she was right. So much oil flowed out of that posthole that Ma and Uncle Seth were able to build a substantial mansion on Lindell Avenue in St. Louis, where they finished raising Marcy, six children of Neva's, and two of Aunt Rosie's as well, the latter having died in childbirth after five years of marriage to a banker in Dubuque.

Marcy had a fine, lilting soprano voice—Ma sent

her to Europe to train it thoroughly, which she did. Marcy sings with the New York opera now, not a form of singing Uncle Seth could bring himself to enjoy.

"Reminds me too much of a Cheyenne scalping party," he said.

G.T. claimed that the horrors of the Fetterman massacre stunted his growth, which didn't matter, since he was already as big as he needed to be. The puppy Sweetbreads gave him lived to be twenty-four years old. G.T. never married. He decided that what the world needed was a reliable supply of catfish, so he started the first catfish farm in Missouri, an enterprise that failed, due to being way ahead of its time. The bankruptcy that resulted made G.T. a bitter man—it turned him into a hellfire preacher. Then his reason slipped and he began to stand in the street and rant about hellfire to the passersby. He even stood right in the middle of Lindell Avenue and preached while visiting Ma—it was a great embarrassment to the children.

As we came east along the Platte after our fateful visit I happened to spot an old tattered law book that had dropped out of some wagon, a good thick digest of laws from all over the place. After I had pored over that old book for a few years I decided to become a lawyer—Ma borrowed the money and sent me to law school in Chicago, over Uncle Seth's loud objections. He was convinced I would become a judge and find against him in court.

"Does a chicken have loyalty?" he asked. "Does a lawyer?"

Lawyers weren't as thick on the ground then as they are now—I not only became a judge, I became the top judge in the whole Missouri judiciary. Luckily Uncle Seth was never in legal trouble, but several of Neva's children took trouble for a middle name. It was just luck that none of them showed up in my courtroom.

You don't have to be long on the bench to realize that family cases are the hardest to settle. Give me murderers and bank robbers any day, over a family that's got crosswise. It's deuced hard to know where a family story starts, and no cinch to figure out where one stops, either. If family cases started with a wedding and ended with a funeral, judges wouldn't dread them so much—but it's rarely that way.

Look at our family, the Cecils. You could argue that the main story started the day Ma shot Sheriff Baldy Stone's horse, under the mistaken impression that it was an elk—but that was just a point on the map of our life as a family. *Did* Ma always prefer Uncle Seth to Pa? *Did* Pa wander the west for years, hoping his brother would relieve him of his outspoken wife? *Did* Uncle Seth mean from the first to steal his brother's wife? Did they all three know what they were doing, or half know, or just blunder on?

I've pondered the matter for many years, but I confess I still can't phrase it out tidily, like you need to do with cases in the courts of law.

Ma took us all that way, through storms and past bears and Indians, just to tell Pa to his face that she meant to quit him. And there's Uncle Seth, who stayed devoted to Mary Margaret Cecil his whole life, although she was never his wife—Ma *quit* Pa but she never went to the trouble to divorce him. Then there was Pa, a sprightly man who survived a hundred Indian scares just to get his head cut off by a snapping blade in his own sawmill, and was buried by his rich daughter, the author, in a fine grave beside the Columbia River Gorge. I remember them all as they were that last night, standing on the parapets of Fort Phil Kearny, all three holding rifles, while that great power moon, like a white sun, shone on the living and the dead.